Copyright ©

All r

The characters and events portrayed in this book are fictitious.
Any similarity to real persons, living or dead, is coincidental
and not intended by the author.

No part of this book may be reproduced, or stored in a
retrieval system, or transmitted in any form or by any means,
electronic, mechanical, photocopying, recording, or otherwise,
without express written permission of the publisher.

THREE NIGHTS IN STOCKHOLM

By Elizabeth Hardy

ELIZABETHHARDY

ONE

Remi already knew the back of a cab didn't work for foreplay, having knocked her head, back, and knees enough over the years. But today, she was hoping she'd at least have enough room to change.

Her flight left in just over an hour, and she was half-dressed on the freeway, looking at way too many brake lights.

Even without a partner, the space was tight, and getting out of her skinny jeans was proving harder than she'd hoped. Of course, it didn't help that she'd dumped her case on the seat beside her to save time.

When her phone pinged from the footwell, she rolled her eyes, assuming it was Chris asking where the hell she was.

"Shit."

Kicking her purse aside, Remi peeked over her knee to see a text lit up the screen.

YOU'RE FUCKING INCREDIBLE.

WHEN ARE YOU NEXT IN TOWN?!

She smirked and dug her hand under the waistband of her jeans. As she lowered her pants, her mind flashed back to the night before.

He'd been surprisingly gentle getting the same jeans down not six hours ago. Remi could still feel his lips on her stomach. His fingers on her thigh.

They were tender at first, peeling the skin-tight denim down her tanned and toned legs, his eyes on hers the whole time. But when they tugged off her feet, he'd pounced, leaning over her with a big dumb grin on his face.

Then his fingers were back. Tracing circles under her knee, getting bigger and bigger until-

"The LIE's a parking lot through to Flushing. Want me to try Queens Boulevard?" the driver called back, keeping his eyes on the road like he was being paid to do.

Remi let out a frustrated breath. "If it's faster. I'm already late."

Her jeans were off, and she was pulling up her pants when she felt the car take the exit. It would be close, but she was sure she'd make it. She stuffed her clothes in her carry-on bag and straightened her tie, turning her attention to her hair.

Slowly, she pulled the hair tie free and ran her fingers through the long dark locks, a tingle running up her spine as she remembered how *his* fingers had felt. They'd been strong and forceful, and he'd grabbed and tugged at her in all the right ways.

When she pulled it back, she could almost feel his face beside hers. The way he'd stood behind her and pulled her hair back, exposing her neck to him, had been intoxicating. His stubble tickled and scratched as he worked his way down to her shoulder, and she'd reached back, slipping her own fingers into his blond curls.

With that, he'd moved in even closer, and she'd felt him against her back.

All of him.

All at once, he'd spun her around, catching her arm and all but dragging her to the bed. He smirked, pushed her back to the mattress, and took his time to look her over.

"Not bad."

"Fuck you."

The jeans were first and then her shirt. He'd licked his way up, hovering over her lips until she leaned up to meet him. She could feel his smile against hers as his tongue moved. She would've been happy to kiss him all night, but when his hand touched her, she melted.

Remi cleared her throat and turned up the air in the back of the cab. She was feeling flushed and needed to keep her cool - it was hot enough outside, and she'd need to run to the gate to make it on time.

No doubt Chris would be pissed, and she already owed him one for Berlin.

The cab pulled up, and Remi thanked the driver, hopping out with her uniform looking good and her purse in her hand. She leaned back in and pulled her small suitcase out, taking the time to lift the handle so she could run and roll.

Luckily JFK was part of the "Known Crew-member" scheme, which meant she could skip the long TSA line.

"You ladies mind? I'm running way behind," Remi pleaded to a group of Cathay Pacific flight attendants.

They graciously stepped aside and let her to the front.

Flashing her credentials, she smiled at the agent, who stayed grim as ever. It took seconds to get cleared, and then she was on the other side, speed-walking toward flight AA1752. Paris bound.

As she hustled past the gates, she thought about the upcoming journey - going over the flight plan in her mind, which she knew Chris would've already filed with Air Traffic Control. He was a good First Officer, and she was always glad to see him on her roster.

Of course, Remi had seniority. She'd been flying for well over a decade and had the privilege to pick and choose her schedule. She would "bid" on the routes she felt like flying the next month and was lucky enough to almost always get her way.

Atlântica Airways was a relatively new airline, and she'd gotten in from day one. They flew exclusively between Lisbon and JFK in the beginning, running cheap deals and overnight flights. They started a Paris route next and then London. When the company was bought just a few years ago, they expanded further than any of them could believe.

Suddenly, they were flying to Athens, Rome, Oslo, and more, adding new flights each year. And Remi took advantage of every single route. In the last three years alone, she'd traveled to more than 50 countries, and she loved every single second.

"I know we don't get paid until the doors close, but damn. This is a little much, don't ya think, *Captain*?" Karla raised an eyebrow but smiled. "Hope he was worth it."

Remi laughed and shook her head, moving past the last of the boarding passengers, keeping her head down as she made her way toward the plane.

Chris was in his assigned seat, scanning the papers for last-minute weather warnings.

"Don't even say it. This one's gonna cost you."

Taking her seat on the left with a sigh, Remi nudged his arm. "Hennessy XO?"

"More like...Larsen XO Reserve."

She let out a low whistle as one of the flight attendants came in for her bag. She nodded and smiled, looking to her First Officer with wide eyes. "Sure thing. My bad."

"He got a name?"

"Probably."

The rest of the passengers boarded. Remi looked over the Flight Release and the Notice To Airmen, scanning for anything related to Paris. The last thing she needed was another airport strike.

Chris had everything more or less completed, but they finished the last checks together. Soon enough, the doors closed, and they were given the all-clear to head for the runway.

"Good morning everyone, this is your Captain speaking. My First Officer and I would like to welcome you onboard today for flight 1752 to Paris," Remi began in her best customer-service voice. "We've been given the go-ahead and are sixth in line for take-off. Please ensure your seatbelts are fastened, and your bags are secure. Turn off any electronic devices and remember this is a non-smoking aircraft. Thank you for flying Atlântica Airways, and I hope you enjoy your flight."

They were in the air within ten minutes, a record for getting out of JFK. Remi took one last look at Long Island before locking her eyes on the horizon. In around 7 hours and 45 minutes, they'd be landing in Paris. The City of Love. She'd have three days to eat, drink, and wander. Something she never tired of.

And then there was Sébastien. Something else she never tired of.

TWO

Remi met Sébastien when she was just 19.

She'd saved up every penny she could for a whole year after graduating high school and bought a one-way ticket to London.

From there, she took a train to Paris and then Belgium, Amsterdam, and Dusseldorf. Finally, she made it to Prague for a while and even got a glimpse of the Alps before she totally ran out of cash.

All she could afford in the end was to make it back to Paris, where she promptly got a job cleaning in a hotel until she could afford a flight back to the States.

Her whole life, she'd wanted to see Paris. She was named Remi after the artist, Jean Rémy. He was her mother's favorite, and his was the only piece of artwork she kept in the house.

Of course, her *Place de Ville* was just a print, but the frame was gold, and she'd found it in a thrift store, lovingly hanging it outside of her daughter's bedroom, so it was always the first thing she saw when she woke up.

She'd passed her love for Paris down to Remi, who was a free spirit from a young age. And though she'd loved Paris at first sight, new friends and lovers took her away on that train to Belgium.

But when she came back, broke and happy, she fell in love all over again. She spent the early mornings cleaning in the hotel and the afternoons walking every square inch of the city. She got a pass to the museums and would visit them all, over and over, taking in the art and the colors and the culture. It was heaven.

That was until Sébastien showed up. He came home from a family vacation, resuming his role as a bartender in the hotel before they met by chance. Their schedules were polar opposites, but one night, Remi came back to the hotel for a drink after a long day in the sun.

She sat at the end of the empty bar, sketchbook in hand. Her sun-kissed skin was practically glowing in the moonlight after an afternoon on the grass. Her nose was kind of red, and her cheeks were flushed.

When Séb returned to the bar from his break, he all but stopped in his tracks. Mouth open. Eyes wide.

Remi looked up, smiling at first but then dropping her head before she gave herself away. She felt a rush of heat but tried to keep her cool.

He brought her a drink and spent the night enthralled. She was just as taken by the sexy Frenchman, slowly adjusting her dress to give him a glimpse of her bra.

Things took a turn for the hot and heavy pretty quickly as they made eyes and grazed fingers, waiting for closing time like a kid waits for Christmas.

Sébastien methodically wiped the bar down, moving between the tables and nodding to the hotel guests as they stumbled out the doors and back to their rooms. Every now and then, he would look back to Remi, keeping his head low and his eyes dark.

She sat at the bar, shifting in her seat, desperately waiting for the other guests to leave. But the last man standing nursed his drink, a cigar in his mouth, and his stance relaxed. He'd been alone all night, but Remi had felt his eyes on her. She was young, tanned, and skinny - though that was down to a lack of funds, not a lack of appetite.

When the man stood, he cleared his throat and started toward her. That was until Sébastien got in his way.

"Autre chose, monsieur?"

Anything else, sir?

He placed himself between the man and Remi, a fake smile on his face but an edge in his voice.

"Non. Merci."

No. Thank you.

Remi watched from the corner of her eye as the man walked to the door. She peeked and saw a look of anger on his face. It excited her to see Sébastien get between them like that.

He stood watching, too. Only his eyes were on Remi.

Finally, they were alone.

He stalked to the door, closing it and securing the lock. Then, without a word, he went to her, taking her face in his hands and pulling her into him. His lips were urgent, and he tasted like cigarettes and red wine.

Remi let go, leaning into his body as he kissed her, moving her hands to his back and gripping his shirt. When she felt his hands on her leg, she shuddered. They were firm but gentle, moving higher and higher, pushing her dress aside until he reached her panties.

Pulling away, Sébastien whispered, "Comment tu t'appelles?"

What's your name?

She smiled and whispered, "Remi."

"Tu es si beau, Rémi."

You are beautiful, Rémi.

She slipped her hands under the waistband of his pants and thanked him, looking up through her lashes. They were close to the same height when she stood up straight, allowing her to wrap her arms around his neck and pull him close.

All at once, his hands were on her. She felt him unbuttoning her dress and then a rush of wind as he peeled it down.

She tugged at his shirt, fumbling with the buttons until he finally pulled it over his shoulders, revealing a tattoo on his chest of a fleur-de-lis and a date beneath. She ran her hand over it, wanting to ask what it meant. But then he was on her, his mouth moving from her neck to her shoulder to her chest.

He pulled her bra down, releasing the left breast from the cup and taking it in his mouth. She felt a surge of heat between her legs as he licked and nibbled.

She tried to reach for his belt, but he held her back, looking her in the eye as he slid his hand low. Remi threw her head back as he moved his fingers, his lips back on her nipple.

He started slow, teasing her for what felt like an eternity before he increased the speed and pressure. Finally, when she was gasping for breath, he pulled away, spinning her around and bending her over the bar.

She heard his belt buckle and tensed at the sound of his zipper.

Sébastien leaned over, putting his lips to her ear, kissing her neck. She felt him between her legs and pushed her butt back a little, inviting him in.

When he entered her, she felt full and wet. She could tell he was holding back after a few slow strokes, so she reached back and grabbed his ass, pulling him into her and whispering, "Harder."

He did as he was told, pushing harder and faster, one hand on the bar and the other on her free breast, pinching the nipple with each thrust.

When he lifted his hand to her hair, Remi arched her back, letting him pull it as he slammed into her.

Then his hand was on her again, slipping over her stomach until it reached her center. It only took a few hard strokes before she came. Remi let out a groan, gasping for air as he kept going, stroking and thrusting until he, too, finally came.

Séb collapsed on top of her, and she could feel the sweat on her back. He was breathing hard, and she heard him chuckle.

"What's so funny?" she managed to get out.

"Not funny. Just…incroyable."

Incredible.

The pair kissed and dressed and stumbled back to his apartment, where they promptly hopped in the shower and made love again.

When they eventually fell into bed, Remi groaned, knowing she would need to be up in just a few short hours. But she didn't care.

She was hooked. Totally and completely infatuated with this smart, sexy, and insatiable man.

Gone were her afternoons in museums and lazy days in the sun. With their schedules, it was the only time they had together, and neither wanted to waste it out of bed.

Sébastien lived in a tiny studio in the 8th arrondissement of Paris. He paid way too much for the space, but when she leaned all the way out of his window, Remi could just about see the Eiffel Tower.

They spent every waking minute together, making love in empty hotel rooms, restrooms, and even in the parks when they felt extra spicy. They couldn't get enough of each other, and Remi wondered a few times if he was her happily ever after.

Of course, good things rarely last forever, and when she got a call from home telling her her sister was sick, Remi had no choice but to leave.

They had the cliché goodbye at the airport and promised to keep in touch.

They would visit and write and call.

They would make it work.

Right?

It was four years before Remi saw Sébastien again. It was her first international flight to Paris as a First Officer, and she was beyond happy to be back.

He was just as sexy and had even picked up a few new tricks.

Thirteen years later and he still held a special place in her heart...and her bed.

THREE

"Bonsoir mesdames et messieurs, et bienvenue à Paris Charles de Gaulle airport. The local time is 11:19 pm, and the weather is a balmy 79 degrees Fahrenheit. On behalf of Atlântica Airways and the entire crew, I'd like to thank you for joining us on this trip. We are looking forward to seeing you on board again in the near future. Please keep your seats until the Capitan has turned off the fasten seat belt sign, and do be careful when opening the overhead lockers."

Remi rubbed her eyes as the flight attendant made the announcement. They were heading toward their gate, and she was having Chris bring them in. He'd been working under her for the last few years, trying to get in as many hours as possible so he could become a Captain himself. But given that pilots weren't supposed to work more than 900 or so hours in a year, it wasn't always easy to log in the necessary time.

As a Captain, Remi was happy to be the watchful eye, especially with someone like Chris. He was young but determined and a stickler for details. He made teaching a lot easier than most, which was why Remi happily added him to her routes when she got the chance.

At the gate, she powered down and sighed. "Shit, I'm tired."

"You don't usually go out the night before a long haul."

Hands on her face, she groaned. "I *know*. And you know I didn't drink a drop-"

"I know, Boss."

She smiled at his simple statement. He knew her well.

The truth was, she didn't *usually* go out the night before a long haul. But last night was different. Last night was exciting. Last night was big and toned and impossible to resist. Last night was...she wanted to say, Adam?

A knock on the cockpit door jogged her back to reality. She reached up and flicked the switch to "unlock," seeing Karla on her small screen.

"You guys need anything?"

Chris stood and stretched his back. "Other than a massage? I'm good."

"Thanks, Karla." Remi smiled, her eyes on her landing checklist.

Paris was their final destination, so they had to wait for the passengers to disembark before going through the Secure Cockpit checklist. Then they could head to their hotel and sleep.

Remi had three days in Paris, and she intended to relax. New York had been a bit of a whirlwind thanks to an old friend's birthday party and a guy named... Andy?

"You seeing your Frenchman?" Chris asked, not looking up as he made notes in the logbook.

"I might be. What's it to you?"

"Nothing to me. I'm just amazed the two of you have lasted so long - with the distance, I mean."

Remi laughed and sighed. "Sébastien and I have an understanding. It's easy and uncomplicated, just how I like it."

The crew walked into the terminal together, finding their particular line to make it through customs faster. The flight attendants were chatting in front as Remi finally turned her phone back on.

Three new messages and a voicemail:

WHEN CAN I SEE YOU AGAIN?

She really needed to remember this guy's name! He seemed pretty eager, which she liked. But she didn't want him to be *too* into her.

The following message made her shoulders slump:

BONJOUR MON COEUR. JE DOIS

TRAVAILLER TARD. DEMAIN.

JE PROMETS.

Hello, my love. I have to work late. Tomorrow. I promise.

There went her night. Séb working late meant some asshole hadn't shown up for work, and he had to cover. He worked in a different, more upscale hotel these days, and he was the bar manager. Though that meant more money, it also meant he had even less free time than before.

"Oui?" the security guard called.

Yes?

Remi looked up and hurried forward, smiling an apology and handing over her passport and ID.

On the other side, she found the crew, and they all made their way to the shuttle, which would take them to their hotel. Shoving her bag in the hold, Remi hopped on board and found her seat, pulling her phone back out to check the last message:

> PLEASE TELL ME YOU DIDN'T GO
>
> HOME WITH ANTHONY? HE'S MY COUSIN'S
>
> FIANCÉ AND SHE'S BEYOND PISSED.

Anthony! Oops!

Tongue in cheek, she replied to that one right away:

> HE BASICALLY DRAGGED ME OUT
>
> OF THERE. YOUR COUSIN WILL THANK
>
> ME ONE DAY!

She didn't make a habit of going to bed with men who were spoken for, but she didn't usually check their Facebook status beforehand either. The way Remi saw it, if they came onto her to the point of taking her to bed, the relationship wasn't going to last anyway.

The shuttle wasn't too busy, so most of the crew, hers and other airlines, spread out. It was late and hot in Paris, and but she was sure the young attendants would be heading out within a matter of hours.

Le Méridien Etoile was just over a half-hour from the airport, but she knew they'd make a couple stops before they arrived. Atlântica Airways had an exclusive deal with Le Méridien, giving them a major discount for flight crews. And since Marriott owned them, they had plenty of options if a Le Méridien hotel wasn't available.

But the other crews had other hotels, meaning it was around an hour before Remi was finally in bed, where she was left to dream of her steamy night in New York and what she hoped would be a sweaty couple of days in Paris.

FOUR

Remi woke to the sound of a car horn. It persisted for what seemed like way too long, forcing her out of bed and to the window.

Across the street, a couple of taxi drivers were having a heated exchange. She watched as arms flailed and fingers pointed. Other cars honked as they drove by, fists shaking out the driver's windows.

Welcome to Paris.

Luckily, the cafe culture in Paris rarely slept, and she knew of at least a dozen decent breakfast spots within walking distance. Though, for Remi, everything was within walking distance. To her, there was nothing better than wandering the streets, making her way along the river, and as touristy as it was, sitting near the Eiffel Tower with a book and something sweet.

She showered and dressed without checking her phone, knowing Sébastien would be sound asleep until almost noon. Plus, she didn't want to see any other texts about her night in New York.

Instead, she threw it in her bag made her way out into the heat.

On her first trip to Paris, it had been warm

and sunny but manageable and even chilly in the evenings. Now, with climate change, Paris was damn near unbearable in the summer - just like everywhere else.

Only in France and most of Europe, they didn't have air conditioning everywhere, which meant she was forced to listen to high-and-mighty Americans complaining about the heat while they mopped their sweaty brows under their stupid baseball caps. They stood out like sore thumbs, and she'd worked hard to distance herself from the stereotype.

Remi had perfected her look over the years, making sure she blended in with the locals rather than screaming foreigner.

She wore a red sundress that just reached her knees with white canvas shoes and oversized sunglasses that hid the fact she'd skipped putting on any makeup. She pulled her hair up off her shoulders, pinning the front pieces just so but leaving her neck clear to feel the breeze.

It always made her laugh to see the young girls visiting Paris with their perfect hair and makeup that no doubt took an hour to achieve. By the end of the hot day, their makeup would be smudged, their brows a hot mess, and their hair nothing but frizz as it stuck to their necks and backs.

Remi learned early that stylish didn't mean layers of foundation and heat-treated locks.

The last piece of the puzzle was her bag. She'd bought it years ago in a sample sale in New York, spending more than she'd wanted to but knowing it would last her a lifetime. Remi slung it over her shoulder, loving the fact that the vintage purse was back in style and that it would set her apart from any tourist with a backpack and bulky sneakers.

And then there was the language.

Remi learned French in high school and became fluent as she lived and worked in Paris. Over the years, she'd kept learning and speaking wherever she could, though she knew people could tell she wasn't native.

Still, it set her apart, and she was careful never to speak English when she was out and about - it was the kiss of death in most places.

"Bonjour," she smiled as she approached the counter. "Un café et…un…" Remi glanced over the glass, biting her lip a little as she tried to make her choice. "…une baguette."

She nodded and pointed to let the guy know she'd be outside. He smiled and all but waved her off. Not in a rude way. Just very…French.

The sun was peaking over the top of the buildings across the street, but there was little to no traffic at that point. She watched people walk their dogs and take their kids to school, sipping on her coffee and devouring the baguette with ham and cheese. Remi always started her day with something sensible and filling, along with a sweet treat which she was more than ready for.

When the waiter collected her plate, she asked for another coffee and something fresh from the oven. He furrowed his brow slightly but returned within minutes with a hot coffee and steaming pain au chocolat.

"Fais attention," he cautioned.

Be careful.

Nodding her thanks, Remi lifted the plate and took a deep breath. She could smell the butter, chocolate, and powdered sugar all at once, and it took everything she had not to dive right in.

Instead, she pulled out her phone and sipped her coffee. To her surprise, she had a message from Sébastien from almost an hour ago:

MON CHOU, J'AI TRÈS ENVIE DE TOI.

JE VEUX TE MANGER. JE VEUX TE BAISER.

OÙ ES-TU?

My sweet bun, I want you so bad. I want to eat you out. I want to fuck you. Where are you?

Remi felt a pulse between her legs and shifted in her seat, imagining his hands on her. Séb was never shy about telling her what he wanted, and she was more than happy to oblige.

In all her years, she'd never known another guy so eager to pleasure her. They'd spent more nights than she could count with his head between her legs and just the thought of it got her going.

With a smirk, she replied:

SÉBASTIEN, JE SUIS TRÈS MOUILLÉE POUR TOI.

JE VEUX SENTIR TES MAINS SUR MOI.

ES-TU EXCITÉ, MON AMOUR?

Sébastien, I'm wet for you. I want to feel your hands on me. Are you horny, my love?

Her phone rang seconds later.

"You kill me, Remi. Where are you?"

"Mon chéri, I thought you'd be sleeping. Tu travaillais tard, tu te souviens?"

You were working late, remember?

"Remi..." he warned.

She felt the pulse again when he growled her name. They hadn't seen each other in a few months, and the first time after such a long break was always rough - in a good way.

"Sébastien," she cooed. "Je mange. Et ce chocolat est chaud et mouiller."

I'm eating. And this chocolate is warm and wet.

"Remi, je jure devant Dieu-"

Remi, I swear to God-

"Tell me what you want. In *English*. S'il te plaît."

He let out a harsh breath on the other end. She knew she was driving him crazy, and the truth was, she wanted nothing more than to race to his place and take his pants off.

But she also knew that the longer she toyed with him, the more she'd be punished.

"Remi. Ma colombe, ma chérie. I have not seen you. My body aches for you. I want to kiss you. I want to put my lips on your skin and hear you moan. I want to put my fingers inside of you and taste you. Remi, s'il te plaît. Je ne peux plus attendre."

Please. I can't wait any longer.

Hearing his need for her was more arousing than anything else he could've said. She could hear how much he wanted her and imagined his hard dick pressing against his pants while he sat there, horny and craving nothing but her.

"Le Méridien. Chambre 202. Fais vite, ou je commence sans toi."

Be quick, or I'll start without you.

FIVE

Luckily, she hadn't walked too far from her hotel, which was a little further from Séb's place than others in the past. So Remi left cash on the table and hustled, knowing she had at least 15 minutes before Sébastien arrived. That gave her plenty of time to change into something she knew would drive him insane.

The airline moved its crew around a lot, so although this and the last trip had been at Le Méridien, she had no way of knowing where she'd be next time. Otherwise, she could let him know in advance.

Although, she kind of liked it this way. It gave her all the power, which turned her on even more. Séb practically had to beg for it.

She raced into the room and tugged the dress over her head, reaching for her bag before it hit the floor. Remi kicked her shoes off and rummaged around until she found the little black piece she'd picked up on her last trip to Italy.

Tossing her undies and bra into the closet, she stepped into the lingerie, keeping the straps apart as it glided up her thighs and over her hips. Then, with the thong in place, she grabbed the straps and placed them over her nipples, being careful to lay each one below just so.

They sat against her like a second set of ribs. Stripes of leather and silk wrapped down from between her breast, curving just above her hips before moving up to her shoulder, leaving the back totally naked.

She lifted the last of them and wrapped the cuff around her neck, grabbing the stockings with her other hand. They were black and clipped onto the bottom of her garter, elongating her slim legs, which were that much sexier in the heels she snatched up from the bottom of her bag.

Finally, she stalked into the bathroom and pulled the clips free from her hair, letting it tumble over her shoulders. Red lipstick was the final touch before she reached for the hotel's bathrobe.

She'd just perched on the edge of the bed when she heard a light knock at the door. Cinching the robe closed, she had to keep from running. Instead, she made him wait a minute, standing with her hand over the door handle while she counted to 20.

"Ouvre la putain de porte, Rémi."

Open the fucking door, Remi.

With a giggle, she pulled the door towards her, revealing Sébastien in all his glory. He wore dark pants with brown shoes and a crisp white shirt, open at the collar to reveal his dark, tanned skin and thick chest hair. Even after all these years, he had a full head of dark, wavy hair, which brought out the blue in his eyes.

When he was younger, he'd been clean shaved. Always. Every day he'd spend too long in the bathroom, running the blade across his strong chin and square jaw, making sure not a single hair remained.

Now, he had a thick beard that he kept clean around the neck and trimmed just right. He was polished and perfect, down to the last button.

When their eyes met, Séb raised his left brow and looked her up and down, noticing the robe and smirking at the heels.

"What, no flowers?" Remi asked, biting her lip.

He lowered his head a few inches, looking at her through his lashes under a furrowed brow.

"Pourquoi as-tu besoin de me torturer?"

Why do you need to torture me?

Remi put a hand on her chest and gave him her best "who me?" face.

"Monsieur. Pardonne-moi-"

Sir. Forgive me-

He raised his hand and put a finger to her lips. She was done talking.

"Inside," he whispered, stepping in, so she got a whiff of his scent.

"Bien sûr," she smirked.

Of course.

Remi walked backward, her eyes never leaving his, which moved up and down as he tilted his head. When they finally met hers, he gave her a half-smile and lifted a hand to his chin.

He brought it to his mouth, running the first two

fingers over his lips while the thumb moved into the hair on his chin. Then, keeping the hand where it was, he lifted his index finger, gesturing for Remi to turn around.

She did as she was told, spinning on one heel. When she faced him again, Séb took a step towards her and gently brushed his hand against the front of the robe, skimming his fingers between her legs and grazing her skin.

"C'est très bon. But I wonder…" he moved his hand further under the robe, reaching for her nipple.

When his fingers hit the strap, his eyes shot up, dark and excited.

"What are you hiding, Remi?"

"Me? Hiding? No, I was just sitting here in my old, ragged sweat pants. Nothing under here but lint and torn seams, I'm afraid."

"Et talons hauts?"

And high heels?

She shrugged and turned, strutting to the window. He stayed where he was, tapping his foot on the carpet. She didn't need to turn to know what he was doing.

He stood with his arms crossed and his brow raised, waiting for her to come to him. But she knew she could hold out longer.

Slowly, she pulled at the robe, opening it a little with her back still to him. Before she had the chance to turn, he was breathing down her neck. Wordlessly, Séb reached around and grabbed the tie. He tugged it free, pulling both ends out of the loops. Next, he put his hands on her shoulders, inching the soft fabric down to reveal the skin, silk, and leather.

"Not so much privacy here," he murmured, his lips at her ear.

The room overlooked the street, and they were only on the second floor. So if anyone were to look up, they'd get quite the show.

"Let them look," Remi whispered, brushing the robe off and turning to face him.

He had to step back to take her in. His eyes wandered over her body, hungry and horny. He still had the tie in his hands which he playfully twirled as he whistled.

"Baise Moi."

Fuck me.

Remi chuckled. "That's the idea." But when she made a move to him, he held up his hand. His eyes locked on hers, and he shook his head slowly.

"Stay."

Her heart fluttered, and her skin prickled. She felt a rush of heat between her legs as he moved into her, slowly and with purpose. His lips touched hers as he caressed her arms. She felt his fingertips move from her shoulders to her wrists until they finally took hold.

Séb took a small step away and brought her hands together in front of them both. Then, using the robe's tie, he began binding her. Over the years, he'd perfected the knot, though they'd never used something so thick before.

It felt good against her skin, though she missed the

rope.

When Séb tugged, her breasts shook, and he leaned in and kissed along the straps, narrowly missing her nipples.

Quickly, he lifted her hands and pushed her back until she all but fell into the window. The cold glass caused her to gasp, but his heat was all she could think about. He kissed her with urgency, his strong tongue slipping in and out of her mouth while his teeth nibbled at her bottom lip.

He kept her hands pinned over her head with his right hand while the left moved across her body. It grazed her inner thigh and ran up behind, following the stockings and landing on her bareback.

Then, just as quickly, he stepped away again, leaving her hot and breathing heavy.

A dark smile crossed his face as he reached up, using both hands to tie hers above her head. The curtain rod didn't seem overly solid, but Séb secured it tight enough that she couldn't move more than a step or two in front.

"Turn around. Laisse-moi te regarder."

Let me look at you.

He moved away, and she obliged, moving slowly and rolling her hips a little. When she faced him once more, he laughed and shook his head before coming to her.

His hands started on her back, scratching gently until they were low enough to cup her plump ass. Remi leaned into his kiss as his fingers moved lower, grazing her warm pussy.

She moved her legs, inviting him in, and felt his laugh on her lips. Instead of going deeper, he moved his hands away, trailing them up her back and under her shoulders until they found her breasts.

"This I like," he noted, feeling the straps and her nipples beneath.

They held her breasts in place, and when he grabbed at one, it fell free. For a second, she felt a cool breeze against her skin, but it wasn't long before his mouth was on her.

He sucked, licked, and tugged until she started to moan. Then he moved to the other. When he stepped back, they were perky and begging for more. Before she could ask, he reached out his hand and stroked the silk covering her mound.

Tortuously, he tucked them beneath the fabric, and Remi let her head fall back. She lifted her hips to him, and his fingers caressed her clit, moving annoyingly slowly. As they reached her entrance, she bit her lip and took in a breath. She could feel how wet she was and knew how much that got Séb going.

He moved closer and kissed her, his fingers working overtime between her legs until she could feel an orgasm coming. Her breath was short as the pressure built, and his fingers started to move faster. She wished her hands were free, so she had something to hold onto.

But just as her moaning was about to hit its peak, Sébastien pulled his hand free and stepped away.

"Pas encore, mon amour."

Not yet, my love.

SIX

"*Sébastien!*" Now it was her turn to growl.

Remi leaned forward, pulling against the rope with a pout on her face. Séb smirked and held up his hands, glancing to the curtain rod.

"Careful," he sang, pointing over her head. "Patience."

Infuriated, all she could do was watch as he undressed, undoing each button as slowly as possible. When he reached the last one, he lifted the shirt free from his tight pants and let it fall from his shoulders.

He'd been in the sun, she could tell. The line around his neck was faint but deep enough that she saw where he'd been dressed and when he'd been shirtless.

As he moved to his belt, he kicked his shoes off, nudging them back before reaching down to remove the socks. All that remained were the pants. Remi wanted to scream at him to hurry, but she knew how much he enjoyed watching her squirm.

"Ça va, Remi?"

You OK, Remi?

"I'm fine. Merci."

Gritting her teeth, Remi put all her focus on his

pants. She'd already felt his excitement, and now it was more prominent than ever. He pushed them down, bending at the waist so he could reach his foot to get them free.

Standing back up, Remi let out a sigh. He was wearing black briefs that hugged his ass the way she liked while giving her a clear outline of his rock-hard dick.

She licked her lips and bit down, knowing what was coming, wanting urgently to reach out and touch it. Of course, he knew exactly what he was doing, and it drove her crazy. Her pussy ached for him, and when their eyes met again after a couple of minutes, she let out a groan.

"Jesus, Séb. Can you just fuck me already?"

He was standing with his hands on his hips, watching her lusting after him. With a slight shrug, he slipped his hands under the black material and slowly pushed them down.

Standing upright again, his cock looked to be reaching out to her. Even his dick looked tanned, and she could see he was freshly manicured. It swayed from side to side as he took small steps her way, stopping just as the tip touched her thigh.

"You want this, Remi? Tell me."

She kept her mouth shut, not wanting to give him the satisfaction. But when he reached up and gently pinched her nipple, she gasped. Still, she tried to stay strong, keeping her mouth in a smirk and her eyes on his.

Séb shrugged again and looked down, moving his

hand to her thigh. It trailed up to her panties and along the lining between her legs. When his fingers touched her again, she could feel she was close. A few strokes, and she was done for.

Expertly, Sébastien moved his hand so he could enter her without touching her clit. She was warm and wet, and he let out a small breath as his fingers moved inside.

"You want this, Séb? Tell me," Remi echoed, her voice catching slightly when he slipped in a third finger.

She thought he was ready to play some more, but apparently, it was too much even for him. He grabbed her shoulder and pushed her around, pressing her up against the window with one hand while he ripped her underwear down with the other.

Using both hands, he pulled her hips to him before placing one hand on her back. She felt him between her legs, his hand guiding his erection, though she doubted he needed it.

He entered slowly, holding himself back at first. But then he lost control and crashed into her, letting out a guttural groan. She matched him with her own cry of pleasure as he moved in and out.

After a few strokes, Sèb moved his hand to her nipple, twisting and pulling.

"Fuck, Séb. I'm so close," Remi breathed, her hands against the glass, still above her head.

"No," he whispered, pulling himself free and turning her to face him.

He was red and out of breath, his cock glistening in

the light from the window. Even as a young man, he'd had incredible control, somehow able to stop mid-thrust when she was screaming for more.

Remi ached, her clit pulsed, and her nipples throbbed.

This was what he wanted. He wanted her at the edge. He wanted her at his mercy.

To her relief, even the master of patience couldn't seem to wait any longer. He moved to her and lifted her up, letting her wrap her legs around his waist. Séb pulled her in and kissed her as he entered her once more.

The glass was cold against her back, but Remi didn't care. She was lost in the movement, feeling him between her legs, his strong arms holding her steady. He thrust up, slamming her into the window each time with a grunt. Remi was gasping, moaning each time he filled.

When he pushed her legs down, she felt a flutter of excitement. She felt him fall out of her as he stepped back and couldn't help but let him see the worry on her face. But instead of teasing her again, he turned her back around and pushed her legs apart. Her breasts touched the window as he thrust his hips up, pulling a loud moan from her lips.

Séb was relentless, rocking his hips as hard as he could, his thick cock rubbing her insides in all the right places. Soon enough, he reached around took her left nipple in his fingers, tugging and pinching as she cried out. Eventually, she heard his breath quicken, and seconds later, his other hand was on her, stroking her clit as he hammered into her as hard as he could. They rose together, and Séb plucked and slapped and thrust harder and harder until she finally screamed out.

Only then did he allow himself to cum. His cry was loud and one of complete satisfaction.

Remi felt lightheaded, still riding her own high as he moved his hand and took a step away. Séb laughed and fell back onto the bed, his dick still hard and soaked in cum.

"Uh. Sébastien? Un peu d'aide?"

A little help?

SEVEN

"Bonjour mesdames et messieurs, et bienvenue à Atlântica Airways. We're delighted to have you on our flight to New York today. Looks like we have clear skies all the way, and we're scheduled to land around five or six minutes early. Please sit back and enjoy your flight. The crew will be serving drinks shortly, and I'll speak with you again once we're closing in on the big apple."

Remi sat back in her seat and sighed, removing the headset and rubbing her neck. Once again, Chris was at her side and ready to take the proverbial wheel as soon as they were at cruising altitude.

"You look refreshed," he commented.

"I am. Thank you. How was *your* time in Paris?"

He thought for a second and smiled. "You know, it wasn't bad at all."

Unlike Remi, who'd spent her youth exploring Paris and all its wonders, this was only Chris's second trip. She had the feeling he'd met someone, but he hadn't said anything yet. So she'd leave it for now and let him tell her if and when he was ready.

The flight was uneventful, and they landed seven minutes ahead of schedule. But, since another was taking over and heading right back out, Remi and her crew had little to do but clean up and head home.

Remi's apartment in Manhattan was small but in a good building on the upper east side. She even had a minor view of Central Park when she stuck her head out the East 85th Street window.

She'd bought the place in the early 2000s, back when real estate prices were high but not astronomical. The apartment had been her aunts, and she got it at a reduced price, her mom giving her a hand with the downpayment.

Aunt Colleen only needed enough for a condo in Florida, leaving Remi with a mortgage that she was close to paying off and an apartment worth close to a million dollars at this point.

In recent years she'd been renting the place out on Airbnb. Working the dates around her schedule wasn't always easy since she didn't know when and where she'd be more than a month ahead. But the beauty of New York City was that she could open a block of dates up on Monday and have the place booked up solid by Wednesday.

She'd never been one to hoard knick-knacks and liked the minimalist look anyway. That made renting it out even more manageable. She had a locked closet where she stored most of her stuff and a cleaner on hand to bring in milk and coffee before a new guest arrived.

On the off chance her schedule changed and she couldn't go home, she would treat herself to a night in a hotel or call up a friend to spend the night.

And over the years, she'd made a lot of friends.

The 7:15 am flight from Paris landed early, and with the time difference, Remi hopped in a cab, knowing it would be close to noon when she'd pull up in front of her building. Of course, that depended on the traffic.

Still, knowing her most recent guests had until noon to check out and then her cleaner would need a couple of hours to come in and change the sheets, she opted to call Susanna. No sense in rushing them out when she could have coffee with her best friend instead, right?

"You back already?" Susanna yawned.

"Yup. And I'm craving something bad. Meet me at EJ's?" Remi let the silence on the other end go for a few seconds before adding, "It's on me."

Susanna laughed and said, "Well then, sure. You in a cab?"

"Yeah. Let's call it an hour."

It was closer to 45 minutes. They made it across the Robert Kennedy Bridge without a single stop, and the FDR was moving well. Before Remi hopped out of the cab outside the Luncheonette, she stuffed her jacket and tie into her purse.

She was left wearing her slacks, shoes, and white shirt. It was a little bit formal for the diner setting, but she didn't care, and she knew nobody would give her a second look. It was New York City, after all.

Inside, she found one of their usual booths and grabbed her phone. She had a text from Séb and a missed call from her sister.

À BIENTÔT?

See you soon?

Two days with Sébastien was never quite enough for him, and he was always extra lovey-dovey after she left. Ironic considering how he liked to fuck. But for Remi, it was just enough. It kept things exciting and fresh, and she liked that she had an excuse to leave.

He stayed perfect that way.

"Early, huh?" Susanna breathed as she swept in.

She was tall and stunning, her blue eyes bright and curious no matter what she was doing. She had shoulder-length light brown hair that fell into perfect waves, and her minimal makeup only made her that much more attractive.

"Can you believe it?" Remi smiled, looking to the counter before her eyes fell on her best friend. "Did I miss something?" She asked with a smirk.

"What?" Susanna asked, feigning ignorance.

Before she could answer, the waitress appeared, coffee pot in hand.

"Coffee?"

They nodded and held up the cups that were already on the table.

"You ladies need menus?"

They didn't, and the waitress knew it. She recognized them, having served them for more than five years. But true to her style, the lady refused to acknowledge anybody as more than a passing face.

"No. I'll have the BLT," Susanna announced, reaching for the sugar.

"And I'll take the French toast with bananas and pecans. Plus a side of bacon and home-fries. Please," Remi added with a grin.

The waitress walked away with no more than a nod, leaving Remi to eye her best friend and the cleavage she'd shown up with.

"So, you heading to a date I don't know about?"

Susanna laughed and sipped her coffee. She played with the strap on the little blue sundress and shrugged. "I might be."

"Jesus, Suse. Tell me already."

Knowing she couldn't hold it in even if she tried, Susanna rolled her eyes and leaned in. "Remember that guy from last year? Troy, from that work thing?"

Remi thought back. "I need more."

"The guy...you know..." Susanna looked to one side to make sure the waitress wasn't hovering close by before adding, "the guy that made me squirt?"

"Oh!" Remi sat back and bit her lip. "*That* guy. Yeah, how could I forget? Wasn't he, like, a male model or something?"

Shaking her head, Susanna took a breath. "He's a trainer, and he did a piece in the Times after Matt Damon mentioned him in an interview."

"So, he's a *celebrity* personal trainer. Sexy *and* loaded."

"In more ways than one," Susanna muttered into her coffee.

"No, no," Remi tutted, wagging her finger. "You

don't get to say that and move on. Details, please."

Taking another quick look over her shoulder, Susanna lowered her eyes and continued, "We went out a couple nights ago. It was totally random - we just ran into each other when I was out with Claire."

Claire was Susanna's work wife, whom Remi didn't altogether love.

"I was at the bar ordering another round of drinks when he just appeared at my side. Said he'd seen me when he came in and just *had to* come over and say hi."

"Ok," Remi started. "But wasn't he-"

"French toast?" The waitress appeared from out of nowhere, stating their order as though she couldn't remember who had what.

"That's me," Remi said, lifting her finger in the air like she was being counted for attendance.

Once the food was on the table, the girls started eating, focusing on their food while it was still warm. Remi devoured the bacon and most of the fried before turning her attention to the pancakes. They were tall and steaming, and she knew she'd struggle to finish.

She also knew that Susanna would finish her sandwich and dig in before long.

"So, Troy. Wasn't he the guy that just disappeared on you?"

"After some of the best sex of my life!"

"OK. I mean, I'm not saying you shouldn't see him. *Obviously*! But, did he give you an excuse?"

Susanna wiped her mouth and finished off her coffee, looking for the waitress and holding up the cup for more. They sat in silence until both cups were topped up, and the woman was back behind the counter.

"He said he just got busy. Some last-minute work thing that took him out west. Honestly, I don't even care. I'm not looking for my first husband here. I just need to get laid, and his dick is a thing of beauty. Plus, he *loves* foreplay."

"Sounds too good to be true," Remi whispered, her eyes back on her food.

"Speaking of…" Susanna let it hang in the air, but Remi didn't take the bait. "Oh, come on. How was lover boy?"

Remi thought about it for a second, her hand on her chin. "Tanned."

"And?"

"And as perfect as ever. In fact, I think he got bigger. His arms felt huge, and my thighs almost hurt after sitting on those hip bones."

"I didn't see you walk in? Did you need a crutch?" Susanna joked, knowing exactly how Séb liked to fuck.

"Not this time."

"And, uh…how's Sophie?"

She'd known it was coming. The second his name came up, Remi knew Susanna would ask about her - she'd just hoped it would be later.

"Sophie's fine, as far as I know. We don't usually discuss her, as you know."

Susanna picked at the fries on her plate and shrugged. "I was just wondering if he ever mentions her. Does he ever have to run away because she's calling? You already said you guys can't leave the hotel or be seen together because he's so well known in that circle-"

"Come on, Suse. Gimme a break. I'm not his keeper. I'm not responsible for what Séb does with his dick. And we've been doing this since we were *kids*. Since-"

"Since before he got married."

Her tone wasn't judgmental or argumentative, but Remi still felt her neck flush.

"Sébastien is a grown man. He can fuck, or not fuck, whoever he chooses. I just happen to prefer it when he fucks me. Plus, he didn't even tell me about her until she called one night. I didn't know, remember?"

"But you still see him. You still go to Paris knowing he's going to be at your door within the hour with a charming smile on his face and his dick in his hand."

"What do you want me to do, Suse?" Remi sighed, leaning back, her appetite gone.

"I just want you to think about this poor woman. She thinks she's happily married to some great guy. What's she gonna feel when she finds out her loving husband is in love with another woman?"

"He's not-"

Susanna cut her off. "Don't give me that shit. It's been like 17 years. Of course, he's in love with you."

"Yeah, well. You *both* know that that's not what I want. I don't want love and monogamy. I want excitement and new men. So, if I have to give up what I have in Paris, so be it."

She could still feel his teeth on her nipples and his hands between her legs. Séb always left his mark on her, though it was usually in the form of a love bite or unusual bruise.

But now, with Susanna asking about his wife after every trip, she was starting to think it was time they ended things.

After finishing their food, the pair parted ways, Susanna promising to spill the tea on her big date with Mr. Foreplay in the morning. When she finally made it home, Remi collapsed onto the bed. The fresh sheets smelled amazing, and the place was perfect - as usual.

Making a mental note to give her cleaner a raise, Remi stripped down and hopped in the shower. She noticed a few scratches on her breasts and a new bruise on her hip.

Séb had always liked to fuck, and he wasn't afraid to show how much he wanted her. Luckily, Remi liked it rough. If she had a dollar for every time she'd had to tell a guy to fuck her harder, she could've retired early. Was it that hard to understand?

The truth was, even though some guys took feedback well, a lot didn't. As a result, she'd lost out on plenty of second dates because she'd gently made suggestions in the bedroom. Although now she was in her thirties, she wasn't as gentle.

Why the fuck should she settle for sub-par dick when she knew what she liked?

Séb knew her. He knew what she liked and what she didn't like. He knew when to push it and when to be gentle. He knew that she liked it when he told her what to do and that, to a point, she liked to be dominated.

But he also knew that she got off on the power, too, and was more than happy to let her have her way with him. He was sexy and familiar and yet, still exciting, even after so many years.

Remi didn't want to give him up. But she knew Susanna was right and that eventually, she'd have to stop being the other woman.

EIGHT

"Hyvää huomenta, and good morning, ladies and gentlemen. Welcome to Helsinki. The current temperature outside is a lovely 24 degrees, and the skies are completely clear. It's exactly 2:17 pm, and we should have the doors open in just a few minutes. Thank you for flying Atlântica Airways, and we hope to see you again soon."

The flight attendant sounded sleepy as she made her final announcement. Remi cracked her neck and sighed, happy she didn't have to put on a fake smile for the passengers. "Is it me, or did that leg feel longer than normal?"

Chris laughed. "You're just getting old. These overnights never used to bother you."

Glaring at him, she muttered, "Little shit."

Even though it meant an overnight flight, Remi loved coming to Helsinki. Not because she liked Finland, but because she liked to take the ferry to Tallinn. Just a couple of hours south, the little city sat right on the coast with its storybook old town and old school charm.

She had two hours to get the passengers off, turn the plane around for the next crew, and make it to the docks. She used to take the long way, opting for the train and a tram. Now, she hailed a cab and paid the €70 to cut the transit in half.

"Hey, boss. Got any plans for Helsinki? The weather looks like it's gonna hold." Her lead flight attendant, Marie, stepped into the cockpit and leaned against the wall as the passengers trooped off behind her.

"I'm actually heading out on the 4:30 ferry to Tallinn," Remi answered, keeping her eyes on her checklist.

"You know, I keep meaning to head down there. Is it worth the trip?"

She thought about it for a second, and a smile spread over her face. She pictured his eyes, broad shoulders, and perfectly sculpted ass. "Oh yeah. It's worth it."

"And it's like, a couple hours on the ferry?"

"Yup. €30 or so."

"Huh. Maybe we'll join you."

Remi smiled, knowing Marie was full of shit. She had her routines in every city they landed and rarely branched out to try anything new.

In Helsinki, she'd visit the cathedral before walking south to the Esplanadi. She'd grab a coffee and a pastry and read her book in the sun. Then, she'd go get a massage and end her day in the sauna. The other two days would be similar; only it would be a different landmark and a different pastry.

After around 30 minutes, the crew finally made their way off the plane and into the terminal, showing their IDs with tired eyes and polite smiles. Out front, the rest of her team boarded the bus with a few other airline crews. Remi waved them off and made her way over to the taxis.

"Hei, West Terminal 2, ole kiltti."

The driver nodded and pulled away, working around the other cars until they were on the main road south. She glanced at his phone, the Waze app showing nothing but green lines. Puffing out a deep breath, Remi leaned back and closed her eyes. They would be pulling up to the ferry terminal in around 40 minutes, and there didn't seem to be any traffic.

That would give her around 30 minutes before boarding closed - plenty of time to make it inside.

Everything was automated, and she'd never spent longer than ten minutes checking herself in. Plus, it was never too full on the ferry. Most of the passengers would be lined up underneath to drive on.

Choosing to keep her eyes closed, Remi let the sun warm her face. It was always tough going from day flights to night flights, and even though the airline gave her a few days to switch over, she never could get it quite right.

After arriving home from Paris, she had a couple of days off before starting a week of short-haul trips to Miami and back. Monday through Wednesday, she flew the roundtrip to Florida every day, then had a day off before doing another three days.

She'd been scheduled to head back to Paris the following week but didn't feel like she could see Séb again so soon after her talk with Susanna. Luckily, since she was one of the most senior pilots at Atlântica, she had the luxury of choosing her routes first and switching where possible. Less senior pilots could only choose after the top dogs had their share.

So, she found a buddy who didn't mind making the switch. Paris was a shorter trip anyway, and he decided to bring his wife along for their anniversary. Much more romantic than Helsinki. It was a win-win for everyone.

Sébastien had been disappointed, but she gave him little choice. He knew the drill: "You see me when you see me. I won't make Paris a permanent route."

Somehow, Remi managed to fall asleep. She didn't feel the car stop, and the driver had to wake her.

"Excuse me? We're here," he whispered, his hand gently touching her knee.

"Shit, I'm sorry. Thank you." Remi reached forward and tapped her card before hopping out.

Inside, she found the check-in confirmation on her phone and used the QR code to scan through to the terminal. There were a couple of bars upstairs, but she knew they would be boarding soon enough. She could grab a Starbucks onboard anyway.

Finding a seat close to the doors, Remi pulled up her messages and hesitated, her thumbs poised to type but her brain not fully awake yet.

Eventually, she wrote:

TERE! I'M IN THE TERMINAL.

LOOKS LIKE EVERYTHING IS RUNNING ON TIME.

AM I GRABBING A BOLT, OR CAN YOU COME GET ME?

She knew that Bolt, which was basically the Estonian Uber, wouldn't cost a lot. But she was hoping this guy was excited to see her.

She hadn't been to Tallinn in almost a year, though he'd come over to Helsinki around six months ago when she texted to tell him she'd be in town. They'd spent a few days in bed before she flew back out, but he'd be *very* into her.

Still, things could have changed since then.

The pair had met in a nightclub in Tallinn. He was tall, with a head of dark hair, and seemed very excited to be there. She'd never seen a guy so into the music, and even though pretty much every girl in his vicinity was checking him out, he was more into the DJ.

Remi being Remi, she didn't want to wait until he noticed her. So, she danced between the bodies and pressed up against him. He looked down at her and smiled, then pulled her in with his big arm around her waist, and they danced until the lights came on.

They'd stumbled back to her hotel and had drunken sex that she honestly couldn't remember. But in the morning, he got up without waking her and went downstairs to get them both breakfast. He snuck back in with two plates overloaded with food and steaming hot coffees.

"Tere hommikust," he smiled.

Good morning.

"I didn't know what you might like, so I got all of it.

And I assumed with the coffee."

Remi sat up and smiled, taking the coffee and laughing a little. "Wow. Aitäh." She nodded.

Thank you.

"Haha, palun," he added, offering her a plate.

Please.

Reaching for a pastry, she said, "So, that was fun... I think."

"Yeah. I don't remember it much, either."

Though neither remembered much from the night before, they more than made up for it after breakfast. Remi put her plate aside and got up, closing the bathroom door so she could pee. Then, she stood and took off the T-shirt she was wearing. When she opened the door again, Risto had his head in his phone. So, she cleared her throat and tossed the shirt out onto the bed.

He glanced up and raised his eyebrows. She stood in the doorway in her underwear, which she promptly removed before turning to the shower.

"There's plenty of room in here, you know," she called out after a few minutes.

He was at her side in seconds, his solid chest pressing up against her shoulders as he reached around and cupped her breasts.

"I'm Risto, by the way," he whispered into her ear.

"Remi," she sighed, turning her head so she could reach back and kiss him.

Needless to say, they both made plenty of memories that day. And she'd seen him a few times over the last couple of years. He was younger but so much fun and was always willing to meet her, even last minute.

When she'd changed her route, she'd texted him to let him know she'd be in town, and he'd responded with a simple, "Okei." Knowing he wasn't much for small talk, she shrugged and assumed that meant it was, in fact, OK.

Before they took off from New York, she'd texted again to remind him, but he hadn't replied. So, standing in line for the ferry, she felt a little nervous that she'd have to spend her time in Tallinn alone.

But just as the ship started moving, her phone buzzed:

VARSTI NÄEME, KULLAKE

See you soon, babe.

NINE

The ferry pulled in on time, and Remi followed the masses across the boardwalk, through the terminal, down the escalators, and out the front door.

Tallinn wasn't usually too warm, even at the height of summer. But when she stepped out, she was met with a wave of heat that was enough for her to take her jacket off.

The sun was shining, and the sky was blue: perfect for a day wandering the city. That far north, the summer days were long, and the sun didn't usually go down until close to midnight. So it wasn't unusual for it to stay warm well into the evening. Something she'd quickly learned as she explored the city, losing track of time with no darkness to keep her on track.

Every time she met Risto, he took her somewhere new. The first day they spent together, he showed her around the Old Town. They roamed the side streets and went into all the little shops before winding up in Raekoja Plats, the Town Square.

They'd found a seat near the edge of the patio and ordered spiked coffees while people hustled around them.

"At Christmas time," Risto said, "We have a big

market here. All the place is lit up, and there are vendors with food and craft. It's quite beautiful."

"Huh. Hope I see it someday."

She still hadn't. Most of the flights Remi took to Helsinki were in the Spring or Summer. It just worked out that way. Still, she'd always wanted to see the place in the snow.

The Old Town was about as picturesque as she'd ever seen, and it looked straight out of a fairy tale. In contrast, other parts of the city were very modern and built up outside the old walls.

Tallinn was a small city that most people had never even heard of. Yet there she was, making the trip from Helsinki every chance she got.

"Don't tell me you didn't recognize me?" a voice said from her left.

She turned and was greeted by a big, beautiful man with a very un-Estonian grin on his face.

"Oh wow!" Remi gushed, putting a hand to her mouth. "It's so short!"

For as long as she'd known him, Risto had sported ear to shoulder-length dark wavy hair. It was very California surfer-esque, and she'd always loved the way he flicked his head to keep it out of his eyes.

Now, it was cut short at the sides, with a bit of length on top. The waves were still there, but it made him look more mature. Was that intentional?

"Sulle ei meeldi?"

You don't like it?

"Sulle...ei...meel..." Remi echoed. The few words he'd taught her hidden away somewhere in her busy mind. "Meeldi-Sulle. Ei. Meeldi-*oh*. No! I mean, no-yes, I like it. Ja."

She shook her head and blushed.

"Mulle meeldib. I *like* it," he offered, raising an eyebrow.

"Ja. Mulle meeldib," Remi repeated, taking a step closer. "It suits you."

"Yeah, well, can't be young forever, right?" Risto shrugged, reaching to her side.

Remi knew he was aiming for her bag, but she took the opportunity to lean in. He was tall, as most men were in the Baltics, and when his fingers touched hers, his lips hovered near her ear. She turned her head just slightly, letting her mouth brush against his.

He didn't react at first, keeping his hands and his lips right where they were. Then he stood up, straightening his back and closing the gap between them, so he was looking down on her from above.

Slowly, he took her face in his hands and leaned in, kissing her gently. She responded by raising her heels. Soon she was on her tiptoes, eagerly reaching for more.

"Don't you want to eat?" Risto whispered, eventually.

Normally, she would have said, 'It can wait. 'But she hadn't really eaten since a couple of hours before the flight. Her body was calling out for food way more than some Estonian sausage - no matter how good it was.

So she sighed and leaned against him. "I'm starving, actually."

Risto took her bag and grabbed her now empty hand, pulling her to the left from where he'd appeared.

They walked across a small street to a parking lot and hopped in his car. Driving in Tallinn wasn't as stressful as driving in New York, and since it was so small, she found they were never in the car for more than 15 or 20 minutes.

From the docks, they took a right, following the road until they came face to face with the Old Town walls. Then, Risto took another right, running parallel to the stone as they crossed over into Kalamaja.

"Did you move in the end?" Remi asked, looking at the cute and colorful houses. Risto had been thinking about leaving his old apartment the last time she'd seen him.

"Yeah. It's in Kalamja, actually. I wanted to be close to work."

"Wait. I thought you worked near Viru?"

"I got a new job. In Noblessner at this Texas BBQ place. That's where we're going."

Noblessner was a newer part of town built on a very old part of town. Where Kalmaja was for the hipsters, Noblessner was for the new money.

Apparently, some big investor had bought up a bunch of land and dilapidated buildings and was in the middle of making it the new most sought after location. Now, there were plenty of expensive new apartments and fancy restaurants on the water.

She and Risto had walked along the coast once or twice, though much of it had still been under construction then.

Risto took a right after a large park, though it looked like they were driving into someone's property. The entrance was bookended by two big white houses, and the small road seemed to hug the wall.

To their left, she saw a huge stone building, and ahead she could see the water. They'd made a ton of progress, and the place looked all but finished in her eyes. Before they reached the bridge to enter the port, Risto took a left around a tiny roundabout before pulling into a small parking lot.

The place was very industrial chic, with a spiral staircase leading up to a balcony packed with locals enjoying the sun. On the side of the building was the word: Põhjala. *Nordic.*

"Wow, Risto. This place looks amazing. How do you say it?"

"Poyella, more or less. They're a brewery," he added, pointing to the end of the street where the building continued. "They have the whole place. I just work in the restaurant."

Remi followed his lead, watching as he nodded and smiled at the staff downstairs. Inside, she could hear that the place was packed. As they made their way up the stairs to the dining room, they were met with huge windows overlooking the brewery. Bottles were moving on the belts, and she saw a few people who seemed like they were tasting something in the far corner.

Upstairs, there was a massive bar with countless beers on tap. Above the bar were TV screens showing the daily offerings, and Remi noticed menus on the bar. Risto grabbed one as they passed, walking straight out and onto the balcony. He led her to an empty table that held a small "reserved" sign in the middle.

"For us?" She laughed, feigning a southern accent. "How sweet."

"Perks of working here." He grinned, handing her the menu. "I'll be right back."

She watched him go inside and lean over the bar. The guy closest turned, and they bumped fists before both turning to look at her. She waved and went back to the menu.

In the end, they shared a whole bunch of delicious food and got a taster of a few different beers. Every now and then, someone would come by and say hi, and Risto would introduce her with a smile. She dutifully nodded and told them all how amazing the place was. Luckily they all spoke English.

When they were full, and all smiled out, the pair strolled down to the water, where they sat for a while, watching the people and the boats. Remi leaned back against him and let the sun warm her skin.

After a while, Risto hopped up, jogging to the end of the strip and disappearing around the corner. When he reappeared, he had two ice creams in his hands.

"Jäätis," he offered.

"Yaaah-tis. Aitäh," Remi replied.

Thank you.

It was almost 9:30, and the sun was dipping. The

sky had turned a stunning pink color, and the whole port was full of people coming to take pictures. Remi and Risto stayed quiet, enjoying their ice creams and the beauty of the horizon.

"So, I meant to ask," Remi said after a while. "You got a girlfriend yet?"

She felt him chuckle against her back and then his breath on her neck. "It's a little late for that, don't you think?"

She shrugged and twisted to see him. "Hey, man. We could just be buddies. Buddies go out to dinner all the time. Buddies can sit and enjoy ice cream while watching the sunset. Where's the harm in that?"

"You want to be buddies?" Risto asked, his hand sliding around her waist. "I don't know. Buddies don't usually fuck, do they?"

Before she could stop him, he slid a hand under her shirt. Luckily, they were sitting on the edge of the water, and everyone around them was more focused on getting the right angles for the 'gram.

"I mean, I've never tried it with any of mine. But there's a first time for everythi-"

Remi gasped as he skimmed his hand beneath her bra and pinched her nipple. She felt him tug at it, sending a shockwave down to her groin. When he pulled away, she felt cold, which she knew he'd been counting on.

Not one to be outdone, she moved her arm behind her back, shifting it between them until her hand landed on his crotch. To her delight, she could already feel him.

Trying to keep as still as possible, Remi pinched his zipper between her fingers and tugged it down. Then she moved between the steel to find his dick all but pulsing at her touch.

"You always get hard when you hang out with your friends?"

He laughed again, and she felt him move away. For a second, she thought she'd gone too far, and he was embarrassed or angry. But then she felt a hand on her wrist and heard him snarl.

"Let's go."

TEN

Risto's old place had been closer to the city center. It was a small studio with a pull-out bed and a tiny bathroom. But the view had been worth it, the windows giving them a clear line of sight to the sea.

Now, apparently, he lived within walking distance of the restaurant. So they walked back toward Põhjala, more or less following their own footsteps under the bridge. But instead of heading back to the parking lot, Risto pulled her to the left, toward what looked like a walled-in park.

"What about your car?" She chucked as he dragged through the gates.

"We'll come get it tomorrow. My place is right up there," he answered, pointing through the trees to where some newer buildings stood. He pulled her closer so she could follow his outstretched finger. "The dark grey house?"

"Oh yeah," Remi mumbled, ignoring the house altogether and pulling him in. "I see it. Seems an awful long way to walk..." she let her words trail off as she reached up to meet his lips.

It was only a few hundred meters, but she'd been ready to go all night. From that first kiss at the docks, she'd wanted nothing more than to have him take her home. And after dinner and drinks and meeting all his coworkers, she'd waited long enough.

On their left was a long warehouse. Earlier, he'd told her that people held raves and parties there, the music blaring until the wee hours of the morning. But right then, it was dark and quiet.

Before he could protest, Remi dragged Risto to the stone, their lips holding on as they shuffled. She felt his tongue curl around her own as his hand tugged at the waistband of her jeans.

Moving a few steps to the side, the pair fell into a small space between the buildings. There was a big door in the middle with a chain and padlock, and a few meters in front, there were trees between them and a path that ran the length of the park. She turned and pushed him against the wood, her hands firm on his chest.

"Remi-" Risto started.

But she stopped him with a finger to his lips. Then, she slowly dropped to her knees and unbuckled his belt.

"Remi. There are people…"

"So we'll have to be quiet, right?"

He opened his mouth to argue, but she was too quick. The second her tongue touched the tip of his swelling penis, he was gone. His hand curled into her hair, and she heard him groan when she took him into her mouth.

"Fuck," Risto murmured as she licked and sucked, using her hand to slowly stroke up and down his length.

When she heard voices behind them, Risto held his breath, still guiding her head with his hand. She could feel his need and knew he wouldn't last long. It gave her such a thrill to know she had this big strong man literally in the palm of her hand. And that any minute they could get caught.

Before he could finish, he pulled her head back. They locked eyes in the dark, and he guided her up, ramming his tongue into her mouth. Moving his hands under her arms, he lifted her and turned, pushing her against the big door before lowering her to the ground once more.

"Let's see how you do with being quiet, shall we?" He smirked, unbuttoning her jeans and tugging them to her ankles.

"I bet I can do-oh, *fuck*!" Remi wanted to be a smart ass, but he was on his knees and pulling her underwear to one side before she could respond.

His tongue was warm and quick, and he didn't waste a second. His other hand was on her, too, his fingers sliding inside with ease.

Remi let out a loud moan and gasped when he sucked her clit in between his teeth. At the same time, his fingers moved skillfully in and out of her, drawing circles around her opening before shooting back inside.

"Fuck," she breathed, feeling the pressure building already. His tongue was quick, flicking over her clit to the same rhythm as his fingers. "Fuck. *Fuck*!" She gasped again when he pressed his thumb to her pulsing mound. "Fuck me, Risto. Now!"

He didn't need asking twice. Risto stood and kissed her, moving his hand from her clit and under her shirt. He pinched at her nipples again before lifting the shirt and bra. When his lips enclosed around it, his other hand returned to between her legs.

This time, the rhythm was slow, moving around her clit and down to her opening before sliding inside for a few strokes. It wasn't long before Remi started to ache.

"Risto…" she warned.

He laughed against her breast and whispered, "Just remember to stay quiet."

Then he flipped her around, pressing her naked chest against the door. She felt his boot between her knees as he gently stepped on her jeans to get them lower. Then, he pulled her hips back, and she felt his still hard dick moving between her slick apex.

Agonizingly slowly, he ran his length across her sex, reaching to the bottom of her clit for a brief second before pulling himself back to the pussy.

He was still teasing her, and she wanted to cry out. But then she heard voices again.

Risto heard them too, but instead of holding off, he rammed into her soaking and aching opening. Over and over, he thrust inside until she couldn't stay quiet any longer.

Remi let out a cry of pleasure the second his hand grabbed at her nipple.

"Oh fuck. Oh…*fuck,* Risto."

He moved his other hand down, reaching around

to her clit as he kept up the pace. She heard his breath catching, knowing he was just as close.

When his fingers pressed against her clit Remi felt the pressure coming to boiling point. He stroked around a few times before he finally gave her what she wanted. His rough fingers all but dragged against her most sensitive area, and she whispered, "Yes. Fuck, yes."

Then he started tapping. It was gentle at first but turned hard the closer he got. The pain and pleasure of him spanking her clit threw her over the edge, and she came so hard and fast, her knees almost buckled. Her stomach contracted, and she twitched her hips as he thrust into her a few more times, finally cumming with a loud groan of his own.

"*Fuuuuuuck,*" he whispered against her ear. "Fuck, Remi."

"So much for quiet," she joked.

ELEVEN

Reaching down, Remi fumbled in her purse for a tissue. She found a pack and handed one to Risto, who nodded his thanks and started to clean himself up. Remi used a few to wipe the cum from her thighs, chuckling at how daring he made her feel.

"Well, I guess someone got a good show." She shrugged, tossing the wet tissues into a nearby trash can.

She heard his zipper and a small intake of breath.

"Lucky assholes."

Once they were both dressed, Risto took her hand and pulled her back onto the path. They walked and talked the few hundred meters to his apartment, seeing only a few people still out in the dark.

"This place looks fancy," she noted as he swiped his fob at the front door. "That restaurant must be paying you well."

He nodded and kept his eyes down. "Must be."

His apartment was on the top floor, and to her surprise, it was modern, bright, and well decorated. She went to the big windows, peering into the darkness towards the sea while Risto went to the kitchen.

"Drink?"

"Mm-hm," she answered without turning back.

After a few minutes, she felt him behind her, his chest against her shoulders once more as he leaned down to kiss her neck. Then she felt a chill on her arm.

"Hey!" Remi cried, moving to one side and taking the drink.

"So, you like the place?" he asked, turning back and taking a seat on his grey couch.

"Looks like you had help," she joked, perching on the edge of an armchair. "Or was your last place just an anomaly?"

"You didn't like it?"

"The sofa bed and tiny shower? What could I possibly have against that?"

Risto nodded again and shrugged a little. "I was young."

"Hmmm." Remi smirked.

Suddenly he was on his feet. He tilted his head and gestured to a door. Remi followed into the bathroom, and her eyes lit up. The whole place was tiled, and the shower was huge, with a rainfall shower head and what looked like freshly laundered towels on hooks, no less.

She immediately moved to the shower and turned on the water. It ran hot almost right away.

"Use whatever you need," Risto started, moving to the sink to grab something from the draw. "Here. This is better, I think," he added, handing her some shampoo that wasn't also body wash.

Remi took the bottle with one hand and gripped

his wrist with the other.

"You're not going to stay and show me how the shower works?"

"Oh, you just…" Risto began.

Remi put her hand over his mouth and shook her head. She reached for his shirt and started to undo the buttons, keeping her eyes on his as she got lower and lower. Using both hands, she grazed his skin with her nails, up and over his pecks until his shirt lifted from his shoulders. Her hands caressed his biceps as the material fell to the floor.

He stood still, watching her slowly undo his belt and jeans, shifting his hips as they shimmied down his legs until he was standing in nothing but briefs and socks. To her delight, she could see he was ready for round two.

But before she could step under the water, Risto pulled Remi to his chest. He held her wrists between them and leaned down to kiss her. It was soft and gentle, his tongue caressing hers with tenderness rather than pure lust.

After a few minutes, the room was starting to get steamy. He ran his hands around her waist, sending a shiver up her body before lifting her shirt up and over her head. Next, he reached around and unhooked her bra, tapping at the straps a little until it fell to the ground.

Her breathing was quick, causing her chest to heave. Risto smiled at them and leaned down again, brushing past her lips and coming to a stop at her left breast, which he lifted with his hand, guiding her nipple into his mouth.

Before, he'd been rough and needy. She'd felt pain and pleasure all at once and got off on his inability to control himself.

Now, he was affectionate and moving with precision.

He trailed kisses down her belly until he tugged at her jeans. They were on the floor in seconds. Not able to wait any longer, Remi threw her hands around his neck and pressed her body against his.

He lifted her as he stood to his full height, her toes a good few inches off the ground.

Back on her feet, Remi put her hands under the top of his briefs, pulling them down and forward, releasing his cock. She put her hand around it and squeezed, drawing a groan from Risto's lips.

Not wanting her to think she had the better of him, Risto put his hand over her wet panties, pressing his palm against her mound and moving it up and down.

"Want to know the best part of this shower?" he whispered.

"Tell me," Remi breathed, moving her hand up and down his length.

His nose touched hers, flicking gently at the end until she looked him in the eye. Remi followed his gaze to the side wall of the shower, which had a steel bar secured in the tile.

There was also what looked like a small ledge for products. It was just the right height, so when Risto stepped under the water and lifted her, she could balance gently on the edge. Remi smiled and reached to her side, grasping the steel bar.

The water pounded them from above, and Risto stood up, his body glistening and toned and gorgeous. Remi reached out and ran her hand through his chest hair, trailing a finger down his abs and along the hairline to his cock.

After a few seconds of admiring her wet body, he reached forward and pulled her panties down. Remi put a toe to the floor and lifted her ass to give him better access.

When she sat back down, she opened her legs, and Risto took a step closer. He grabbed her right leg, lifting the ankle to his lips. The angle forced her to lay back, exposing herself to him further. He reached to her cheek and rubbed his thumb over her lips until she opened her mouth and took him in. She licked and nibbled until he pulled it free and slowly traced it to her left breast.

Circling the nipple, he lowered her leg and brought his other hand forward. His fingers found her again, and she shuddered under the heat of the shower.

When she was all but begging for it, he pulled both hands free and came in close. She watched him brace his bare feet before grabbing his ever-growing dick. Again, he played with her, rubbing her until she moaned.

In the park, they'd both been in a rush, desperate to touch and fuck and cum. But in the shower, they kissed and caressed as he moved slowly up and down. When he finally entered her, it was slow and steady. He gave her every inch, filling her over and over again.

She kissed him on the lips, cheeks, and chest, taking his nipple this time with gentle bites. The faster her breath came, the harder Risto pushed it. His cock was so slick and hard it hit every single nerve on its way in and out.

But Remi needed more.

"Let's go to the bed," she growled into his ear.

Risto raised an eyebrow and smirked, picking her up, so his dick stayed put. He raced to the bedroom, but before he could toss on the sheets, she dropped her legs and shoved him back. Risto sat on the edge, dick standing to attention and a half-smile on his face.

Remi took her time, stalking towards him and raising her knees until she was straddled across his lap. She danced and ground into him, rubbing her clit against his dick and lifting her tit to his mouth. He used his teeth then sucked it in, his tongue merciless as she groaned.

After a minute, Remi reached down and pushed his cock in place, raising her hips to allow him entry. Then, as quickly as she could, she dropped her ass, taking his whole length in seconds.

"Ah, fuck!" Risto called out.

He put his hands on her hips as she lifted and dropped, working him harder and faster until he couldn't focus on her nipples anymore.

Not wanting to give up control completely, he swiftly stood and rammed her into the wall. His hands shifted under her ass as he pounded into her pussy as fast as he could.

"I'm gonna cum," he breathed eventually, his

finger dancing around her asshole.

With one hand still on his shoulder, Remi let go with the other and slipped it between her legs, knowing he had to hold on to keep them both from falling. She could hear his breath turn to a pant, so, rather than playing with herself, she went straight for the clit, rubbing it in rhythm with Risto's strokes.

It didn't take too long, and after just a couple dozen more thrusts, they both screamed out in satisfaction. Risto pressed her back against the wall with his final blow, lowering his head as he tried to catch his breath.

"Jesus, Remi."

She took his face in her hands and lifted it until she could see his eyes. He looked tired, happy, and totally spent.

She kissed him again, wrapping her arms around his neck. He lifted her gently, and she felt him pull free, still hard and dripping with their juices. When her feet touched the hardwood, she kept a hand on his arm for support.

After, they both showered properly and wrapped up in the towels. Risto finished his drink while Remi peed and brushed her teeth. A few minutes later, he came back into the bathroom and stood in the doorway, watching as she tried to brush out her wet, unwashed hair.

"What?" she asked when she saw him.

"Nothing. It's just...you're fucking incredible, Remi."

She smiled and turned to him, tugging at the towel he had wrapped low around his waist.

"Trust me; the pleasure was all mine."

TWELVE

"Wait, you had sex in a public park?" Susanna demanded, lowering her voice to keep from being overheard.

Remi nodded and raised her eyebrows, blushing a little at the memory.

"What's his name again?"

Letting out a small sigh, Remi replied, "Risto."

"Risto. Risto," Susanna repeated, rolling the 'R just like he did. "And he speaks English?"

"Oh yeah. Basically perfect English."

They both went quiet when the waiter arrived, thanking him for the food before returning to Remi's hot night in Tallinn.

"So, how did you get to that point? You both must've been pretty fucking horny to stop in a park."

"Oh, Suse. He's just so fucking sexy. The hair, the eyes, the butt. And that dick!" she added, picking up a thick steak fry. "I could eat that dick every single day and still want more. I swear, the second I saw him, I wanted to jump him. And then he takes me to this restaurant, and he's introducing me to all these people. I don't know. Watching him laugh and be totally confident and at ease...I would've fucked him in the bathroom if I didn't think he'd get fired for it."

"But you held off for what, hours?"

Remi nodded, spearing an asparagus stalk with her fork. "*Hours*, Suse. And then," she continued, moving closer and dropping her voice even further. "We're sitting by the water, surrounded by people, and he shoves his hand up my shirt."

"What?" Susanna sat forward, her eyes wide and inviting.

"Yeah. Under the bra, pinching my fucking nipples. What was I supposed to do?"

They both laughed and took a few bites. Susanna was a little more reserved than Remi, but she loved to hear the stories. Not that she didn't have her own tales to tell, of course.

"So, he's up your shirt, and then what?"

"He says we're going back to his place, right? And then he drags me into this park and pulls me close, pointing to some building across the way. But all I can smell is him. And all I can think about is getting my lips around his thick, *beautiful* cock. So, I pushed him into the building and dropped to my knees."

"Wait, so you didn't actually..." Susanna looked around before finishing, "*fuck* in the park?"

"Oh, we fucked in the park. He was so goddamn close, and then he basically lifts me up like I weigh nothing and slams me into the wall. Then *he's* on *his* knees, and his tongue is a thing of beauty. I don't think I lasted more than a minute or two before I was pretty much begging him to fuck me. And he did. He really did."

Remi was getting hot just thinking about it. In fact, she'd been hot thinking about Risto and his cock for the last few days. More than once, she'd caught herself daydreaming about the way his rough fingers felt against her sex. The way he'd lifted her in the shower and entered her so slowly.

That night, she'd woken up to him spooning her. His arm was around her waist, and she could feel his breath on her shoulder. It was sweet and intimate, and she'd loved every second of it.

But, as always, it came to an end. They spent the day in Tallinn, wandering the area around his apartment and fucking on his new couch with the blinds wide open.

Later, he ordered them dinner and casually asked about her schedule. Remi told him she didn't know when she'd be back in Helsinki but that she'd try to make it soon. He shrugged and nodded in his signature hard-to-read way, and they didn't talk about it again.

They went out for a few drinks, and he made her cum three more times before she had to leave for the ferry. By the time she got back in his car to leave, her clit was all but humming from the attention.

Luckily, traffic was light, and they arrived early, pulling into the almost empty lot.

"What time does the ferry leave?" he asked, unbuckling his seat belt and turning the engine off.

"Uh," Remi said, pulling her phone out and finding her ticket. "Oh, in like an hour." She smiled and put the phone back, feeling sort of awkward at having to say goodbye.

"So, you have time?" Risto muttered, reaching his hand over and resting it on her thigh.

Remi blushed and bit her lip, wanting nothing more than to mount him right in the front seat.

"I think this is a little bit *too* public. Don't you?" she asked, looking around. Though there weren't any other cars around, it *was* daylight, and people were milling towards the ferry on foot.

"I can be discreet," he whispered, tucking his hand under her pants.

She wanted to resist. She wanted to shake her head and be an adult. But then she felt his fingers hovering over her mound, and she knew she was helpless.

To his credit, he didn't go any further until she gave him the all-clear. Then, together, they unbuttoned her jeans, and she moved forward in her seat to give him better access.

Somehow, he was able to reach down, tucking his fingers under her panties. They slipped into her sex, going around her opening as she tried to widen her legs in the small space.

Remi dropped her head back when he circled back up to her clit. He worked around it, crossing over only once every few strokes. As he moved, she carefully put her hand under her shirt and bra.

Teasing herself, she felt Risto increase his pace, the whole length of his fingers moving across her mound as he reached again for her opening.

Remi lifted her hips slightly, giving him access to her damp pussy. His fingers were inside within seconds, swirling around as the palm of his hand moved over her pulsing clit.

She pinched at her nipple as his strokes came harder and faster. Turning her head, they locked eyes as he licked his lips, watching her writhe under his touch.

Risto didn't let up. He moved harder and harder until she couldn't hold off any longer, cumming in his hand with a cry.

She wanted to kiss him. To take off her pants and fuck him in the car.

But she knew better. The last thing Remi needed was to miss her flight because she'd been arrested for public indecency.

Now it was two days later, and she was still thinking about him. Even Suse seemed to be infatuated.

"I seriously don't know how you do it. How you can just walk away from *that*. He sounds perfect!"

She thought about Séb and their time over the years. She thought about the men she'd met in London and Berlin, Tokyo and even Sydney. They'd all been gorgeous and sexy, and they all *seemed* perfect. But none of them had ever been good enough to make her stay.

"They're all perfect," Remi mused eventually. "Until the next guy comes along."

THIRTEEN

Three months later

Remi sat at the bar, nursing her diet coke and wishing it had rum in it. Having been on time for her flight to Stockholm, she was now, in fact, four hours early.

"Captain Scott?" the voice on the phone had asked. "There's been an issue with your plane in Reykjavík. They had to remove the passengers, and they're running behind."

So, with a sigh, Remi tossed her phone back into her bag and looked around the pilot's lounge. As always, it was dark and all but empty. A couple of pilots were sleeping on the recliners, but there were no other crew members around.

Choosing to wait in the terminal, Remi grabbed her things and found a bar she liked. No sense in starving, right?

"Hey. How's it going?" she asked the bartender, pulling up a seat near the end.

He smiled at her, and she noticed his eyes moving to her breasts. "Hey, great now. How about you? Delayed?"

With a small shrug, Remi nodded and asked for a diet coke. The guy hesitated a little, his eyes lingering on her smile. She ignored him and pulled out the menu. He was tall and cute, with deep brown eyes and a tight-fitting shirt. But she didn't shit where she ate, and airport staff of any kind was a big no-no, no matter the country.

When he came back, she asked for the burger before he could start up a conversation. He gave her a half-smile that said, OK, *I get it,* and turned to put her order into the computer.

This was her first trip back to Stockholm in a few years. One of the other senior pilots always requested the route because he had family in the city, and between her lovers in Paris, Tallinn, Berlin, and London, Remi didn't mind missing out.

But when it popped up last month, she figured she'd give it a try. Maybe she could cross another city off her fuck-it list?

"Hey, can I get a Kronenbourg, please?" s voice to her side asked with a slight accent.

She looked over to see a very tall blond in dark jeans and a grey sweater. He was wearing brown shoes and carrying a briefcase. She noticed his carry-on at his feet and a light jacket over the handles.

Leaning on one arm, he nestled his things on the seat to her right, lifting his blue eyes to hers. He smiled, and without warning, she felt something in her stomach knot up. As he held her gaze, and Remi was totally caught off guard at the instant attraction she felt.

Or, maybe she was just horny.

"Hello," he offered, his eyes locked on hers as the bartender came back with his drink.

"Anything else?" the guy asked, leaning forward to break their stare.

"A menu, please."

Remi turned back to her drink and bit her lip. *Fuck* he was sexy. She took a sip and tried to come up with something clever, but a waiter intervened, stepping between them with her food.

"You got the burger." It wasn't a question, and he didn't wait long enough to hear her response.

"Looks good. I might need to get the same," the man beside her noted. Though his eyes were on her and not the food.

She licked her lips and gave him a half-smile, her eyes moving to his biceps and down to his ass, which was slightly arched back as he leaned on the bar.

"Maybe I should try it first. Just in case."

Not one to be shy, Remi lifted the big burger and took a bite, enjoying the bacon and cheese with her eyes closed. She'd had it before and knew it was good, though this time, she could tell someone else had made the truffle mayo.

"Oh yeah. You should get the burger." She laughed, wiping her mouth and reaching for a fry. "It's better than sex."

"I somehow doubt that very much but, I guess I'll have the burger, then," he announced loud enough for the bartender to hear. He lifted a hand to acknowledge the order, choosing to stay closer to a group of college girls who'd just walked in.

Trying to be subtle, Remi looked the handsome stranger over. Tall, muscular but not overly so, well-dressed and well-spoken. He seemed a little flirty, too, his eyes searching hers for a reaction with each stolen glance.

"I'm tempted to ask if you come here often, but judging from your outfit, I'm guessing you do," he said all of a sudden, taking a seat and pulling her away from her increasingly dirty thoughts.

Remi looked up from her plate and smirked. "What makes you think this isn't just some sort of cosplay thing?" She brushed her fingers across her right breast, pulling the shirt just an inch as she spoke.

Normally, she would've played it slow. Let the guy talk some to see if he actually had anything to say. But for some reason, with this guy, she wanted things to move faster.

"Good point," he admitted, sipping at his beer. "So, you're...Sully?"

With a chuckle, Remi turned, so she was facing him. She straightened her back, knowing she'd unbuttoned her shirt at the top already. If he looked close enough, he'd see her lace bra under the white cotton.

An image of him on top of her flashed across her mind, and she had to clear her throat before answering.

"I'm just a pilot. A delayed pilot whose plane is stuck in Iceland, apparently."

"Me too - the plane thing. Not the pilot thing."

Fuck, Remi thought, deflating immediately. He wasn't airline staff, but he was one of her passengers - another line she'd never crossed.

"Ah," she began, unconsciously turning to face the bar again. "Sorry…I…"

"It's not your fault, is it?" He lifted his eyebrows and reached out his hand. "I'm Mats. Heading home after a conference in the Big Apple."

She hesitated at first but figured it wouldn't do any harm to talk to the guy.

"Remi Scott. Pilot trying to get you home after a conference in the Big Apple."

His hand was warm but firm, and she felt him squeeze her fingers slightly, lingering for a few seconds before letting her go. They both took a sip of their drinks, and Remi chose to stay quiet, focussing on her food until the waiter brought out Mats 'burger.

He took a bite and let out a small groan. "Good choice," he said with a thumbs up.

For a while, they both stayed quiet, enjoying their food and the slightly awkward silence. Every now and then, they made eye contact and smiled before Remi finished and pushed her plate aside. The bartender came by for a refill and offered Mats another beer. He happily said yes.

"Why not, hmm?"

"So, what was your conference?" Remi asked once they both had fresh drinks. She leaned on the bar and tilted her head, looking up at him through her eyelashes.

"Oh, it's very boring, I'm afraid. Economics,

politics, and the climate crisis. Heavy stuff."

"Wow, sounds…tiring."

Mats thought about it and smiled. "Yes, it was. I've been doing this for many years, but it doesn't get any easier to sit and listen to hours of lectures when there's a city to explore and…beautiful locals to meet."

If anyone else had said it, Remi would've rolled her eyes. But the combination of his subtle accent, piercing eyes, and tight ass made her involuntarily lick her lips.

"Did you at least get to have any fun in the city?" Remi turned in her chair, so she was facing him again. She crossed her leg and leaned an arm over the back of her chair. The movement pulled her shirt open slightly, giving him a better view of her right breast.

"I…uh…like to walk. I go to the park and along the river. Though it's not as beautiful as Stockholm."

"No?" She chuckled.

"Have you been before? To Stockholm?"

"I haven't, actually. Well, no. That's a lie. I've been on a quick turnaround once or twice. I've never seen the city, though. I hear it's nice."

Mats finished his food and turned to face her. He opened his legs casually, leaning an elbow on the bar with his hand on his beer. Remi shifted to mirror his stance and started running her hand slowly up and down the side of her glass.

"It's more than nice," he said, risking a glance at her chest. "I hope you get to explore on this visit. Or is it, as you said, a turnaround?"

Remi caught the glint in his eye and held back a

smile. "I have a day. We were supposed to arrive early and then leave early the following day. That's usually enough time to see the highlights."

"The highlights," he echoed, looking up to the ceiling. "The old town, yes? And maybe a river tour?"

"I was just planning on hitting the streets. Wandering and eating - see what all the fuss is about."

"The fuss?" he asked, his brow furrowed.

"Yeah. I'm curious if it's really as..intoxicating as people say it is. Stockholm Syndrome and all that, right?"

She could see he was about to explain exactly how the name came to be, but he caught her sly smile and chuckled.

"Right. And who knows, maybe you'll meet someone and never want to leave."

His words sounded friendly enough, but the look in his eyes said something else. She started to feel warm around her collar as his eyes took her in. Taking the chance to do the same, she zeroed in on his thighs. They were thick and pressed against his pants. A cyclist? He didn't look like a gym nut, though he did look to be in good shape.

When he shifted, her eyes moved up to his crotch, where a slight bulge made her clit twitch.

"Maybe, but I'm kind of hard to please. It takes a lot to impress me, I'm afraid."

"You don't look so tough. I think if you gave me a day, I could please you."

Another look, another pulse in her groin.

"Is that so? How would you do that? *Please* me?"

She put her elbow on the bar and leaned, resting her chin on her fingers.

Mats put a hand to his own chin and made a show of thinking about it. He rubbed his stubble a little and pursed his lips before offering, "You said you like to walk and eat, yes? My apartment has a beautiful riverside walk just minutes away. Great restaurants too. And I have to admit…I love to eat out."

That caught her off guard, and Remi raised her eyebrows. Gently, she licked her top lip before biting down on the bottom one. Then, she nodded and took a sip of her drink before lifting her eyes to his again.

"Sounds like you'd be quite the tour guide."

Mats moved forward in his seat, drifting closer over the chair that sat between them. "It would be my pleasure to try to please you, Remi."

She noticed his eyes dip to her chest, so she took her elbow off the bar and tucked it to her side, pushing them toward him like an invitation. She uncrossed her legs, brought her hands together on her lap, and leaned in, knowing her tits would now be on full display.

"You sound pretty confident. I might just have to take you up on your offer."

"I hope you do," he said, moving another few inches closer. "After all, what better way to get to know a city? I know all the best places to visit, where you'll feel it touch you."

The truth was, Remi didn't think she could wait that long. She'd never felt so drawn to anyone before, and it was all she could do to keep her hands to herself. She'd been picturing him naked since he sat down, and the closer they got, the more she wanted his hands on her.

"You think a day is long enough to be…touched?" Remi challenged, shifting in her seat. Her pussy was starting to ache, and she could feel she was getting wet just at his words.

"As you said, I'm pretty confident. I don't think I'll have any trouble figuring out how best to touch you."

His hand lifted, and she held her breath as he moved it to her thigh. He kept his eyes on her, asking for permission with a raised eyebrow. She gave him a half-smile and took a deep breath, sliding forward in her seat, moving his hand up a few inches.

In her head, they were already in bed. His hand was between her legs, and his dick was pressed against her.

But they were at the goddamn airport. Not exactly conducive to a spontaneous romp. Remi racked her brain, wondering if they had time to head out to a hotel. She could see he wanted her just as bad, the bulge in his pants more prominent than ever.

Just as she turned to call for the check, her phone buzzed on the bar.

"Fuck," she muttered, rolling her eyes and bringing it to her ear. Mats kept his hand where it was, even as the bartender came over.

"The checks, please."

"Yeah, this is Remi Scott," she said into the phone, trying to focus on what the guy was saying.

"They can't fix the plane in Reykjavík in time, but there's another coming in from Toronto. You and your crew will take that one to Stockholm, so you're not too delayed. It'll be there in an hour."

Frustrated, Remi finished with the man on the phone and slumped in her seat.

There goes the hotel...

"Looks like we got a plane," she said, her eyes on his hand. "It'll be here in an hour or so. So...I gotta go find my First Officer and prepare for the flight."

Mats sat back up and shrugged. "That's a good thing, I suppose. It just means we'll be in Stockholm sooner than we thought."

Remi smiled and paid her tab. Mats ordered another beer, and the pair said an awkward goodbye with a firm handshake. She could feel his eyes on her ass as she walked away, and when she turned back, he was still standing, hands in his pockets and a smile on his face.

It was a sign, right? She was *this close* to walking out of the airport and finding a hotel with this guy. And then, all of a sudden, they had a plane. It had to be a sign.

Don't shit where you eat, she reminded herself, taking one last look at his crotch. *No matter how fucking sexy the guy is.*

FOURTEEN

"Good morning, ladies and gentlemen, and welcome to Stockholm. The local time is 11.33 am, and the weather is a brisk 3 degrees. On behalf of Atlântica Airways, I'd like to apologize again for the delay. Thank you all for understanding, and we hope you have a safe onward journey."

Once they were safely at the gate, Remi slumped in her seat. It had been a long ten hours, and the delay in New York hadn't helped. The only saving grace was that the airline had found another plane, so they weren't *too* delayed.

Of course, a few passengers had missed connecting flights, and no doubt they were pissed. Luckily, that wasn't in her job description.

She worked with Chris on the post-flight checklist, but when she heard the big door open, she couldn't resist. She left him to it and hurried to open the cockpit door, adjusting her tie and tits before pulling it in.

"Hey, all good?" she asked Tony, one of the flight crew.

"Yeah. I mean, I think a few people are gonna be hella mad. At least we don't have to handle that shit, right?" he muttered through the side of his mouth.

The pair nodded and thanked their guests, who mostly smiled back out of habit. She heard Chris speaking with the ground crew and glanced back into the cockpit. They'd been delayed, which meant the next flight was delayed too. She could just about see people watching from the terminal, their faces pressed up against the glass, waiting to be called for their own boarding.

"Thank you so much, Captain," a familiar voice said.

Remi turned back to the cabin to see Mats standing in front of her. He was wearing the jacket now, his polished look complete. Somehow, even after the long flight, he managed to look incredibly fuckable.

"Thank you, sir," she replied with a slight smile. "Have a nice day," she added as he passed by.

He turned back for one last look before rounding the corner, and Remi cursed herself. She should've given him her number back in New York. He could've been her Stockholm tryst - her distraction for the next couple of days. What a waste of good foreplay.

"Boss?" Chris called from behind, pulling her back to reality. "The tower wants you on this."

Dragging her feet a little, Remi went back into the cabin, slid into her seat, and lifted the headset back in place.

"Captain Scott, here."

"Hey there, Atlântica. We've got a cold front coming in, so we need to know if that issue in Reykjavík needs another set of eyes."

Grabbing the technician's notes, Remi responded, "They didn't tell you? This airbus came to us from Toronto. I think the other plane's heading back up north by now. Besides, it was a fluke, Tower. A bird got stuck under one of the elevators, apparently. Either way, this girl's good to go."

Chris rolled his eyes as Remi finished up. In the cabin, the crew tried to turn the plane around fast for the waiting staff at the gate.

"You think we need to worry about the storm?" Chris asked eventually as they all left the plane and headed up to the gate.

"Looked like it was going to veer north. My guess is we'll get a cold front and some flurries, but it won't hit. Besides," she added, stepping into the terminal and nodding at the next crew, "we're only here for a day. I bet we'll be gone before anything major happens."

Together with her team, Remi smiled and passed through security. The cabin crew was quiet for the most part, tired from the delay and overnight flight. They patiently waited their turn before following the crowds to the taxi area. As soon as they stepped outside, the chill woke Remi up, and she took the opportunity to look around.

It wasn't anywhere near as busy as JFK, but it was modern and well lit. Taxis were lined up neatly, and people had room to drop off loved ones across the street. There were no car horns or people yelling. No men in fluorescent shirts moving stragglers along with whistles and harsh words.

Definitely not New York.

"Excuse me, miss? I think you dropped this?"

Remi stopped and glanced down where she saw a gloved hand holding out a card. Confused, she looked up.

Mats took a step forward and added, "You might need it. Or, I *hope* you'll need it."

He smelled amazing, and his eyes were so bright in the daylight. With him so close, she realized he was a lot taller than she was, and she had to strain her neck to look up at him. When he smiled at her, she felt like she was right back on that barstool, her clit throbbing and her mind racing. He seemed to be on the same page and took a small step her way, closing the gap entirely.

"So, that offer for a tour guide is still good?" she asked, tilting her head a little.

"It was all I could think about on that flight. I think my dick swelled every time I heard your voice over the speakers."

Remi bit her lip to hold back a grin and shook her head. How was he doing this?

"Really? I hope you weren't too uncomfortable. It was a *long, hard* flight after all."

He put his hand on her cheek and leaned in closer. "Did you even give me a second thought, Captain?"

Stretching up to him, Remi could feel his warm, minty breath on her nose. "Well, I was a bit distracted up there, and," she looked around to ensure nobody was close, "it was all I could do to not come back and drag you into to bathroom."

Mats moved quickly, his lips meeting hers with enthusiasm. Remi melted into him, leaning against his big firm body. She slid her tongue into his mouth and groaned when she felt his arm reach round her waist.

When he finally pulled back, Remi had to take a breath and hold onto his arm for support.

"I'd like to fuck you now. If that's OK with you?" he asked, brushing his lips against her ear.

On her left, the crew were getting in line to board their minibus. She looked back up to his piercing eyes and nodded.

"You got a car?"

He grinned and moved back, grabbing his things in one hand and offering her his free arm. Remi slipped her hand into the crook of his elbow and glanced back to Chris.

See you tomorrow, she mouthed. He laughed and shook his head in disbelief before jumping onto the hotel-bound bus.

FIFTEEN

Mats drove a well-maintained Mercedes. It was silver and looked to be no more than a couple of years old. She didn't know the model but could see it wasn't cheap.

He dutifully took her bag and nestled it in the trunk beside his own before shrugging out of his jacket and tossing it on top. Remi did the same, pulling her tie away and opening the top few buttons on her shirt. She felt the cold on her chest, her nipples hardening at the excitement of it all.

After leaving him at the bar, she'd stopped in the bathroom to find her panties damp and her pussy needy. It took a few deep breaths, but she finally managed to stand and shake him off.

Or so she thought.

She'd fantasized about their interaction at the bar the entire flight. It killed her to know he was sitting somewhere on the plane, so close but untouchable.

Now, watching him recklessly load the trunk, the flame was more than reignited. Briefly, she looked around and thought about climbing into his backseat. It was more than big enough for the both of them, and she could get it out of her system sooner rather than later.

But when he closed the trunk and locked his eyes on her, she knew it had to wait. This was going to be too good for a backseat.

"Is it far?" she asked, trying to sound casual. Her breath floated in the air in front, and she wondered if he could see her nipples through the shirt.

"It's about 45 minutes if the traffic is OK." Mats stalked her way, reaching behind and resting his hand on the small of her back. "Can you wait that long?"

Remi lifted her right hand and placed it on his chest. She traced a finger down to his stomach and along his belt. When she moved it further down, she looked up to meet his eyes. The back of her hand grazed over the front of his pants, and she felt him twitch.

"Can you?"

She saw him glance at the back seat, but voices from the road made them both see sense.

"No choice." She shrugged, walking around to the passenger side of the car.

Mats climbed into the driver's seat, and they were on the road within minutes. Remi pressed her thighs together, wishing she was wearing a skirt for easier access. She could tell he was speeding but couldn't focus on the road with him so close.

He kept quiet, his eyes moving from the rearview to the road ahead. The car flew in and out of the fast lane, and they were at the edge of the city within 15 minutes.

Then they hit traffic. The car slowed to a crawl, and

Remi smiled when she noticed his white knuckles on the steering wheel.

"Tell me what you want to do to me," she whispered, her eyes low as she turned in the seat.

Mats let out a breath and trained his eyes on her. "I want to take that shirt off. Slowly. One button at a time until it falls away."

Remi pushed her shoulders back, feeling the button strain against her chest. Then, with one finger, she trailed down the front of her blouse, between her breasts and back up to her mouth.

"What else?"

The car inched forward, but Mats managed to keep his focus on her.

"After I take off your blouse, I'm going to get rid of those pants. I'll slide them down your legs with both hands, falling to my knees, so I'm face to face with what I'm hoping are black panties."

She smiled and shrugged. "Could be."

"Next, I want you to undress me. To take your time with it, so we're both teetering over the edge."

"I think I can handle that," she breathed, leaning closer, gently laying a hand on his thigh.

The car moved again and took a corner, still traveling at a slow enough pace for him to keep most of his attention on her.

"Once we're both in our underwear, I'm going to take you to my bed. It's big, the sheets are soft, and I want to see you right in the middle. I'll start at the bottom, kissing your ankles and calves before working my way up those thighs. But I won't stop there. I'm going to reach for those incredible breasts you've been teasing me with since New York."

Remi laughed and looked down at her chest. "What? These?" She carefully unbuttoned the shirt just enough to give him a better look at the black lace. Placing her hands underneath, she lifted them and sighed. "I guess they are incredible, huh?"

Just as Mats moved his eyes back to the road, Remi tugged on her left cup. Her breast popped out, and she waited for him to notice. He'd taken a left, and his eyes were glued to the traffic.

When he finally looked her way, she felt him tap the breaks.

"Jesus, Remi." Mats did his best to look away, the traffic moving more freely now.

Remi laughed and popped her other breast out, making circles around her right nipple with her finger. After a few minutes, they pulled up to a red light, and he abruptly came at her, bending over the center console and binging his mouth down onto her chest.

She felt his tongue swirling while his free hand cupped the other breast. He pinched her nipple, and she gasped and leaned her head back against the glass. Mats stayed where he was, sucking and tugging until she started to feel an uncomfortable ache in her groin.

The car behind honked his horn, and Mats left her side of the car. She felt a rush of cold air on her wet, hard nipple and giggled. Tucking her tits back into the bra, she reached over and found him solid as a rock beneath his pants.

"Don't," he warned, his eyes on the road and the car to his right. "We're almost there."

Sure enough, the car slowed and pulled into the driveway of his building not five minutes later. They moved through a set of gates and below, coming to a stop not far from the entrance.

Mats got out and rushed to her side.

"Let's go."

Remi heard the edge in his voice and bit her cheek. He took her hand and almost dragged her to the elevator where, inside, he kept her at his side, their hands touching as he fumbled for the right key.

The second the elevator doors opened, he was out, hurrying them both to the last door on the left.

His hands were on her before the door closed behind them.

SIXTEEN

"This might not be as slow as I promised," Mats warned in her ear.

"Just fuck me," Remi replied, pulling his mouth to hers as they toppled back into his immaculate apartment.

Mats guided her through to the bedroom, where he managed to control himself long enough to kick off his shoes. Remi did the same, her eyes greedily taking in his profile.

Stepping forward, Mats leaned down and kissed her again, only this time it was more gentle. She felt his fingers against her chest as he deftly unbuttoned the last few buttons of her shirt and pushed it to the ground.

Then, as promised, he removed her pants, using both hands sliding over her ass and down to the ground. When he lifted her foot to take them off, he kissed her ankles, pulling the socks free too.

Back on his feet, Remi moved straight to his pants. The belt came free with a single tug, and when she unzipped the pants, she felt them fall open from the strain of holding him in. They dropped to the ground, and he removed his shirt, dragging it over his head in a matter of seconds.

Before he could touch her, Remi turned to the bed. She bent over and placed her hands on the edge, slowly crawling into the middle with her ass in the air. His hand reached out and touched her, grazing between her legs before pushing her over, so she was on her back.

Mats climbed on top, forgoing the teasing and resuming his worshipping of her nipples. Under his weight, Remi could feel his dick against her leg. She reached between them and took it in her hands, rubbing over the briefs before finally slipping her hands under the elastic.

He was big. Big and throbbing and desperate for her.

"Fuck me," she repeated, grabbing his head and pulling him in for a kiss.

Mats pulled back and smiled. "Like I said. It's my pleasure to please you, Remi."

As he said her name, he moved his hand under her panties and into her soaking wet pussy. They were inside in seconds, stroking at her G-spot with such precision, she thought he'd been given a map.

After a minute or so, he moved up to her clit, clamping down on her nipple at the same time, sending shockwaves from her groin to her tits. He worked around her mound, narrowly avoiding the little nub with each stroke.

When he was sure she was close, he pulled away and moved down the bed. Pulling her panties down, he hesitated at her pussy, and for a second, she thought he might've changed his mind. She sat up, propping herself on her elbows.

Then his tongue was on her, and she fell back, crying out in pleasure.

But he was just as close. After a minute or two, he crawled back up and took his cock in his hands. She felt him between her legs as he licked her lips.

"You want this?" he asked with a smirk.

"Fuck, *yes*."

He entered her slowly at first, taking his time as she stretched out to accept him. Luckily she was plenty wet already, and he moved in and out with ease. It wasn't long before Mats picked up the pace, grabbing her wrists and holding them above her head.

She tried to lean up and kiss him, but he held her back.

"I want to see you," he panted, watching as she moaned and squirmed beneath him.

His pace got faster and faster until he started to slow again. Still moving, he released her hands and whispered, "Tell me what you like."

Remi responded by putting her hands on his chest. She shoved him back and on his side, gasping when his dick fell free. She wasn't empty long, though.

In one swift motion, she mounted him. Remi reached between them and grabbed his cock, guiding it inside as she fell down. She swirled her hips, catching her clit every now and then, drawing a small intake of breath each time.

Mats used his long arms to fondle her breasts and pinch at her nipples. He watched in awe as she rode him, moving faster and faster as the pressure built.

Remi closed her eyes and threw her head back, loving how full he made her. Then his thumb was on her clit, and she knew she was close. He worked at her quickly, moving in time with movements, his pressure getting rougher with each stroke.

When she looked down, she could see he was just as close. His grip tightened on her breast, and he tugged at her nipple as her cries came quicker.

She moved up and down as fast as she could, lifting her ass, so his whole cock slid along the entire length of her pussy. All the while, his fingers dragged across her mound. Then, a few seconds before reaching her peak, Mats used his thumb and forefinger to pinch at her clit. The pain and pleasure she felt paired with him tugging at her nipples sent her over the edge.

She screamed his name as she shuddered her orgasm, rising and falling still as came. He cried out too and grabbed her hips, thrusting up with a groan.

Mats fell back, spent and tired, his eyes closed and his arms wide. Remi lifted herself off his slick cock and lay down beside him, her head resting on his bicep.

"I wanted to do that the moment I saw you," he said through staggered breaths.

"I wanted to fuck you on that bar." Remi laughed and turned so she could face him.

After a few minutes, once they could both breathe again, Mats opened his eyes and smiled at her. "You are so sexy, Remi."

"Shucks. You're gonna make me blush." She

laughed again, sitting up and looking around for the first time.

"I don't think much will make you blush. You practically flashed the man in the car beside us."

"He couldn't see anything past your head."

Mats sat up and put his hand on her breast. Gently, he leaned in and took her nipple in his mouth again. She softened into him as his tongue swirled over the sensitive skin.

"I just couldn't help myself," he whispered eventually, moving up, so his lips were level with hers. "I still can't."

Remi kissed him, pulling him in close and climbing onto his lap.

"I think we could both use a shower and some food. But don't expect to leave anytime soon. I'm going to make the most of that pussy while I can."

SEVENTEEN

Remi showered while Mats went to grab their things from his car. She washed away the long flight, the sweat, and the cum, before reaching for a thick towel and stepping out onto the warm tile.

She heard the door open and saw the steam move as the colder air swirled in. Remi opened the door to see Mats, arms full and face flustered.

"It's freezing out there," he shuddered.

"It's warm in here," she offered, dropping the towel and turning her back to him.

Remi sashayed to the washbasin and bent over to wipe the steam away. Seconds later, she felt cold hands on her hips. They circled around her body and cupped her breasts, sending a shiver down her spine.

Behind her, Mats nestled his head into her neck, and she felt his cold nose trailing down to her shoulder.

"Fuck," she complained. "You are cold!"

He turned her around and stepped back, taking her in as he removed his sweater.

"You said it was warm in here, no?"

She shrugged and watched him undress. In the heat of it all, she hadn't had the time to fully enjoy the view. So now, in the steamy bathroom, she let her eyes trace his outline, the curve of his pecks, and the firm edges of his stomach. She watched his hands as they opened the jeans and pulled them down.

His cock popped up, unbound by briefs. When they were both naked again, Mats tilted his head and reached out. He lightly moved his finger around her nipple, scratching a little as he followed down her stomach.

Just before he reached her mound, he looked up, his eyes hot and heavy. She licked her lip and moved her right leg, giving him better access.

Keeping his distance, Mats slid a single cold finger between her legs. The cold made her nipple stand up to attention, and she let out a small gasp.

But he didn't come closer. Instead, he used a single finger, moving it back and forth as he watched her react to him. Remi's breathing started to come faster, and he finally moved close, dropping to his knees and lifting her right leg. He draped it over his shoulder and let out a sigh of appreciation.

Kissing her inner thighs, Remi tensed. She knew what was coming, aware of how unstable she would be on just one leg.

Mats moved closer and closer until, eventually, his tongue played over her clit. He circled it, toying with her until taking her in his mouth. He sucked and licked over her most sensitive area until he felt her shudder with satisfaction.

Remi looked down as he moved his mouth away. She felt his fingers back in place, and their eyes met.

He worked back and forth, watching her the whole time until he moved to her entrance.

As he slipped a digit inside, he kept his eyes locked on hers. His tongue found her clit once more, and he started to move in time to his strokes.

Remi gasped as he sped up, this tongue working her right to the edge.

One finger turned into two, which became three, filling her and massaging along the ridged inside. At the same time, his mouth cupped her, dragging his rough tongue up and down.

She could feel her orgasm was close and grabbed the edge of the counter for support. But Mats didn't let up. He started to flick his tongue, faster and harder until Remi stuffed a hand in his hair and pulled.

When she came, she cried out and gasped, her leg twitching on his shoulder. Intuitively, he moved his head away but kept stroking inside as she came down and caught her breath. Then he stood and kissed her. She pressed into his chest and reached between his legs. He was still hard.

"What are we gonna do about that?" she asked, her eyelids heavy.

Mats opened his mouth to reply, but Remi put a finger to his lips. She turned and moved a step back, bending over the sink so he would have full access.

He put his hands on her hips, and she heard him say something in Swedish. Stepping close, she felt his dick on her thigh as he leaned over and kissed her back.

Then he put his hand into her pussy and massaged

her opening before moving his cock in place. He entered her quickly, thrusting in so fast they both let out a groan. Remi put her hands on the counter as he put one in her hair. She felt him grip and tug, arching her back as he hammered into her from behind.

He spoke again, the Swedish unfamiliar, but from his breathing, she guessed he was close.

Mats let go of her hair and leaned over, reaching around until his fingers found her clit once more. She was still sensitive, which he instinctively knew. So instead of pushing it, he worked around, building the pressure with each thrust.

Before long, they both came again, Remi putting a hand on the wall as he slammed into her for the last time. His head fell to her back, and they stayed like that for a few seconds, breathing heavily and totally spent.

Eventually, he pulled himself free, and Remi stood, turning around and taking him in again. He was possibly the sexiest man she'd ever seen. And he somehow seemed to know exactly what she wanted and when she wanted it.

For a fleeting moment, Remi wondered what it would be like to fuck him every day. To come home to that cock and those fingers and feel him inside her as often as possible.

Quickly, she shook the thought away. This was a one-day thing, right?

EIGHTEEN

Freshly showered, Remi warned Mats that if she didn't eat soon, she'd turn into a monster.

"Trust me; it's not pretty."

He laughed and glanced outside. "It's going to snow soon. Maybe we should go out now?"

Remi looked to the big windows and furrowed her brow. She saw lots of lights, the river and walkway, and luckily, no neighbors peering in. He was on the top floor, overlooking smaller buildings and the water. Across the river, she saw more buildings and lots of green. It was stunning.

But she didn't see snow.

"Is that, like, a Swedish thing? You get tingles when winter's coming?"

He moved in close and kissed her. "I get tingles when you're cumming."

Remi laughed and shoved him away playfully. Padding to his balcony door, she braced herself and stepped out into the cold.

"Fuck me. I didn't think it snowed when it was this cold?"

Mats stood in the doorway. "It's warming up. The snow's coming. Trust me."

The pair settled on heading out, both wrapping up in preparation. Though Remi still wasn't convinced. She'd seen a cold front coming close but moving north. The snow was supposed to miss Stockholm altogether.

Out on the street, Remi tucked her arm under his and walked at his side. They'd already agreed to stay close to home, and Mats knew an excellent pizza place not five minutes away.

They were seated right away and had beers in their hands before they had a chance to look at the menu. Of course, it *was* only 3:30, so the place wasn't exactly packed.

"So, what's good here? Is there some special I should try?" Remi asked, her eyes greedily taking in the menu.

Mats sighed and blew out a breath. "I always get the pizza. It's not New York good, but it's good."

Remi smirked. "Don't worry. I'm not a pizza snob. Actually," she whispered, leaning in close and looking around to be sure no one was listening, "I much prefer the pizza over here. The authentic stuff. Just don't tell anyone, or they'll take my New Yorker card away."

They both ordered pizza and another beer each. A few people came in from the cold, but the place stayed mostly empty.

"So, have you lived around here long?" Remi inquired, looking out the window. The river was gleaming under the lights, and it looked a helluva lot cleaner than the Hudson.

"I moved to this apartment a couple of years ago.

The market here is a little different to anywhere else, so when a place like mine opens up, you have to jump fast."

"Different how?"

He pursed his lips and brought his hands together. He looked like a teacher getting ready to give a lecture. "In Sweden, you have to be on a list to get a home. It's mostly renters here, and people need to put their names on lists in order to be considered for an apartment." Mats stopped to take a drink and held up his hand, showing her four fingers. "I'm on four lists, and I was number six for my place. Luckily, the five in front turned it down."

"Oh, so it's like, first come, first served?"

"Kind of. The first people get offered the place, and they just work their way down until someone says yes."

"And I'm guessing there's more than half a dozen people on these lists?"

Mats rolled his eyes. "Oh yes. A lot more."

"Lucky you got it. That place is gorgeous...from what I saw."

"Ask me how long I've been on that list," he said with a grin.

"How long have you been on that list?"

"About fifteen years."

Remi almost spat out the beer. "What?"

"A lot of parents put their children on these lists when they're born, ready for when they're older."

"What the fuck? That's crazy!"

"That's Stockholm."

When the food came, Rem's eyes widened. It was as good as Mats said, and they happily ate in silence for the first few slices. Outside, they heard the wind pick up, and the snow started to fall.

"Fuck me," Remi breathed.

"Here? Now?"

"No, look!" She pointed and narrowed her eyes. "You *are* a Swedish wizard, huh?"

"I just know my city. And this is nothing new."

Remi took another bite and watched the snow, hoping they were just seeing the edges of the storm. If it got any worse, there would be a lot of delays.

"What time is your flight tomorrow?" Mats asked, seemingly reading her mind.

"10:30. I'm supposed to be taking the turnaround on the same schedule as our flight today."

"So another pilot will come in and stay one night, then leave in the morning on this turnaround?"

"Yeah," Remi sighed, grabbing her phone to check for any updates.

"Hmmm. I wonder if I should come with you to the airport. The last pilot worked out so well for me. Maybe I'll get lucky twice."

Her eyes shot up, and she raised an eyebrow. "You think you could get *this* lucky twice? I don't think so, pal. Although," she added, finishing her beer, "I bet you and Captain Steve would have a lot in common."

"I've never had a Steve before. Maybe it's time I broaden my horizons." Mats finished his last slice of pizza and pushed the plate back, leaning his arms on the edge of the table. "Do you have someone waiting for you at home?"

The question seemed to come out of nowhere, and Remi wasn't sure what to say at first. She looked to the window and back before answering, worried as the snow seemed to get thicker.

"Why would you ask me that?"

"Well," he began. "A beautiful woman like you. I can't imagine you spend much time alone."

With a shrug, Remi dropped the crust of her last slice to the plate. She pushed it away and mirrored his stance. "With my job, I sort of have to spend a lot of time alone. I go all over, and I have to spend days at a time away. Every week. Not too many guys like an absent housewife. Who would make their dinner?"

"I'm an excellent cook, in case you were wondering."

She smiled and bit her cheek. This guy was too good to be true.

"I don't really do the long-term thing," Remi started slowly. "I have a few men that I see and have fun with, but I'm not really into the relationship thing. It gets too complicated."

Remi could see he knew what she was doing. His eyes looked right through her, and she thought he was going to call her out. But, instead, he lifted his hand to call for the check.

"We should go before this gets any worse."

Out of nowhere, the light snow had turned into a heavy blizzard. She heard the wind whipping around, and suddenly she struggled to see the river.

Fuck, she thought.

Remi paid the check, and they grabbed their things, turning their collars up and putting their heads down. She kept her hand under his arm as he led them home in silence.

Before dinner, she'd assumed that she'd stay the night, have sex a couple more times before kissing him goodbye and heading back to the airport. It would've been the perfect way to tick Sweden off her fuck-it list.

But she hadn't counted on feeling so drawn to him. She couldn't have known she would feel so infatuated.

Of course, she meant what she'd said at dinner. She *didn't* do commitment, and she liked her life and the men she fucked. She also liked hopping on a plane and flying thousands of miles away when they got too clingy.

But the more time she spent with *this* guy, the more she didn't want to leave.

NINETEEN

"You mind leaving those on the tray?" Mats said as she removed her boots, pointing to a small plastic shoe tray near the door.

"Sure thing."

He went into the bathroom and came back with a smaller towel. They'd both gotten cold and wet in the snow, which was starting to settle on the ground.

"I'm gonna make a quick call. See what they're saying about this."

He nodded and removed his sweater. Remi watched him take his shirt off and start on his pants. She got a glimpse of him in his briefs before he turned towards his closet and out of sight. Oddly enough, she wasn't so cold anymore.

Turning her attention to her phone, Remi called the European office for Atlântica Airways. She gave her identification number and flight info and waited as the young girl checked on the status.

"Captain Scott? They're saying the snow will be thicker than they thought, but you're still flying as of right now. But I'd expect a delay if I were you. If it gets any worse, we'll e-mail or call, OK?"

"Ok." Remi sighed. "Thanks."

Mats was still in his room so, Remi took the time to look around. The place was huge. The open concept made it look twice the size, and it was very modern and expensive looking. Either he had exceptional taste, or his ex did.

Bored of snooping, she moved a little closer and heard him speaking. Assuming he was on the phone, Remi went to the kitchen and filled the kettle. The cold had seeped in, and the last thing she needed was to get sick. She had to look through a few well-stocked cupboards, but she eventually found two cups and a box of tea.

"You making two?"

"Of course," Remi said, turning to see him pulling on a hoodie. "Everything OK?"

"Yes, I just had to call into work. Looks like I won't be going in tomorrow."

"Right. Yeah, they said I'll probably be delayed."

Mats came to the island, resting his hip against the granite. He folded his arms and crossed one ankle over the other, looking totally at ease and ridiculously sexy.

"You're not canceled?"

"Nope. They're saying it's gonna let up." Remi poured the hot water and dipped their teabags, wondering how best to approach leaving. "So, uh..." she started, handing him a cup. "I should probably head out - make it to the hotel before this gets any worse. At least then I'll be there to catch the minibus back to Arlanda."

He blew on the hot tea and nodded. "Makes sense. I mean, it would make sense *if* you were still going to be flying tomorrow."

"If?"

"I'm a wizard, remember? I can pretty much guarantee you won't be flying, so..." He put the cup down and closed the gap between them. He draped his arms around her waist and pulled her into his chest. As he ducked his head lower, she had an overwhelming desire to bite his bottom lip.

"You should just stay," he whispered, moving his lips to within a couple inches of hers.

"But...I-"

"You should stay," he repeated, moving close enough that she felt a tickle on her bottom lip.

She wanted to hold off and be strong, but she couldn't help herself. Remi kissed him, running her hand through his hair until she had enough to grab on to.

Pulling his head back, she breathed, "Are you sure? I just don't want to-"

He stopped her with a finger to her lips. Resting his forehead against hers, he took a deep breath. She had a hand on his chest and could feel his heart pumping.

What's happening?

"Stay," he whispered again.

How could she say no to that?

TWENTY

They finished their tea on the couch, sitting close and watching the snow through the window. Remi heard his phone buzz and shuffled away, so he could pull it out of his pocket. When he read the message, he frowned.

"Shit. I have to work a little bit."

"Ok. I always have a book with me," she announced, getting up and tiptoeing towards her suitcase. "I've been dying to start this one."

He squinted his eyes as she showed him the cover of a young woman's silhouette looking out a big window. "Looks Scandinavian. Very gloomy."

She came closer and handed it to him, taking off the still damp sweater. She laid it over a chair and grabbed another from her bag.

"An Easy Target," Mats read. "What's it about?"

"Oh, just a woman hunting down rapists."

He handed the book back and raised his eyebrows. "Sounds...interesting."

"My friend gave it to me. She said it was great. "Gritty" was her word, I think. I like the writer, anyway."

Mats held up his hands, grabbed his laptop, and

lifted his legs onto the big coffee table. Then he patted the seat to his left. Remi took his offer and sank back into the plush cushions. She curled her feet under her butt and leaned up against the side, a big pillow under her body and another behind her back.

She was almost eight chapters in when he finally let out a breath and closed his computer.

"OK. All done."

He put the laptop back in his bag and turned to face her, lifting his leg up and resting his hand on his knee. "How's your book?"

"Well," Remi said, folding the corner of a page and tossing it onto the coffee table. "The main character just cut some asshole's dick off. So..pretty good." She laughed and put her hand on his arm. "You get everything done? I don't mind if you-"

"It's all finished," he said, waving her off. "No more work."

"Hmmm." Remi put a hand to her chin and tilted her head. "I guess we could watch a movie?" she suggested, uncurling her legs and placing her feet on the ground.

"We could," Mats replied, putting a hand on her thigh. He pulled, lifting her leg up and dragging her closer. She tucked it into the couch cushions behind him and lifted the other, encircling him between her thighs. "Or not."

He kissed her softly, caressing her tongue with his as he gently ran his hands up her legs. They made their way around her back, and she felt him place his palms against her hips just before he lifted, falling back and bringing her down on top of him.

Remi moved the hair out of her face and ducked her head, trailing her tongue over his lips before kissing him deeply. She let her body rest against him, his hands on her ass as they made out like teenagers.

Then she felt him twitch beneath her.

Luckily, the couch was big, giving them enough room to move. Remi brought her knees up to his sides and found purchase, raising her torso and pulling away from his lips. She reached down and lifted his hoodie, grabbing the T-shirt beneath it at the same time. Inching it up, she pushed until it was under his shoulders.

With him trapped in the fabric, Remi bent down and licked his right nipple, looking up to gauge his reaction. Mats responded by quickly tugging the hoodie and T-shirt off, giving her full access.

She started slow, licking each gently as he squirmed and chuckled. When she took one in her mouth and sucked, he let out a groan, and she felt his cock twitch through the sweatpants. Not wanting to overdo it, she climbed back up to his lips, grinding her hips against him as she moved.

He put a hand on her arm, but she pulled back and stopped him.

"Oh no. I'm in control here," she whispered, teasing him with her lips but ducking her head before he could reach.

She kissed his chest and his stomach, licking along the waistband of his pants. When she lifted them, she let her finger run the length of his briefs. Not wanting to delay her own pleasure, Remi grabbed at both and shuffled them down his legs. She left them at his knees, her focus now on his erect penis.

Deciding to tease him just a little, she nuzzled her nose against his balls, flicking her tongue against them and drawing sharp breaths from her captive. Remi wrapped her hand around the base of his cock and lifted it, teasing the tip with her tongue before moving down, licking it from tip to base and back again.

When she took the head in her mouth, he moaned. She smiled and took him deeper, sucking lightly and moving her hand up and down the rest of his length.

Keeping a slow and steady pace, she alternated between sucking and swirling her tongue. Every time she ran it over the tip, he gasped, entangling his hand in her hair.

She felt a slight pressure on her head, knowing that he wanted her to take him all in. She breathed in deeply through her nose and let him guide her down, moving her tongue as she took him in as far as she could.

A couple of thrusts was all she could manage, but she stopped herself from gagging. Instead, she gripped the base harder, using her hand to give him pleasure from the top to the bottom.

Moving faster, she felt his cock swelling in her mouth. He was close, she could tell. Another minute went by, and she felt his hands on the side of her face. Finally, he lifted her head and breathed, "Come here."

She did as she was told, wriggling up his body until

their lips met once more. Then Mats rolled them both over, his lips never leaving hers until they were steady and he could lean on his hands.

Like she had, he brought his knees up and grasped her sweater. He lifted the fabric, tugging it over her shoulders but stopping before it fell free. He held it down, her arms trapped inside as he bent down to her breasts.

Using his free hand, he pulled the bra down, freeing her tits to him. He wasn't as gentle, taking them in one by one, sucking and nibbling until she started to wriggle beneath his body.

He had one leg between hers and the other on one side. All at once, he started to move, pressing his big thigh against her groin, still sucking on her nipples as he moved.

Amazingly, Remi felt a pressure swelling inside. If he kept this up for long enough, she knew she'd cum. But she felt that familiar aching inside. She felt empty and wanted desperately for him to fill her.

As if on cue, Mats let go of her arms and turned his attention to her pants. He wrenched them down, taking each leg out and tossing them onto the floor. Then, he put his hand under her right knee and pushed it up, exposing her to him.

Bending to meet her, she felt his fingers glide over her sex. When his tongue joined in, she arched her back and groaned. But he was teasing her, coming close to her clit, but stopping just short with each pass.

Following his lead, Remi put her hand into his hair

and pulled his head. She felt him laugh against her, and then he finally gave her what she wanted. The second his tongue touched her, he slipped two fingers inside. He moved quickly, racking them in and out as he tortured her clit with harsh, rough strokes.

Somehow, he managed to get his free hand up to her breast, where he grabbed at her and found her nipple, tugging and pinching as her breaths came faster.

"Fuck me," she begged. "Mats, god, fuck me."

He didn't need to be asked twice. He moved like a cat, climbing her body and entering her in one stride. Staying on his knees, he lifted her body and shoved a cushion under her hips for support. The new angle made it feel like he was driving even deeper, and when he grabbed her right leg and stretched it to the side, she knew he had full access to everything she had.

Reading her eyes, he reached his thumb to her mouth and slipping it inside, letting her suck and lick until he pulled it free and started to trace circles around her clit. Then, as if he suddenly got a burst of energy, his hips moved faster and his thumb pressed against her most sensitive spot.

It wasn't gentle but needy and rough. And she loved it. The feel of his want for her. The feel of his whole length inside of her.

She heard him breathing, already so close. But she was too far gone. He kept his thumb firmly on her clit, rubbing it without mercy. She came hard in no time, rolling over and over as he sucked at her nipple and kept his hand between her legs.

She felt pleasure and pain, the feeling overwhelming her. Her orgasm seemed to go on and on until she couldn't bear it a second longer.

He felt her start to pull away and removed his hand. Using it to find purchase, he thrust into her a few more times. When he came, Remi was practically humming.

Her pussy throbbed, and her clit was as sensitive as ever. So much so that she shivered when he pulled himself free and grazed past it.

"Remi? You OK?"

She tried to breathe. Her mind was fuzzy, and her heart was pounding. She closed her eyes as her ears started to ring. When she opened them, she saw Mats, looking gorgeous and worried.

"Remi?"

She put her hand on his cheek and whispered, "Let's do it again."

TWENTY-ONE

The sound of her alarm broke the silence in the bedroom. Remi scrambled to her phone, tapping at the screen with her eyes half-closed, hoping to stop it before it woke Mats. She glanced over her shoulder to see him sound asleep still and closed her eyes again.

Fuck, I hate mornings.

As quietly as she could, Remi slipped the covers back and padded out to the living room, closing the door behind her. It was 7 am. She'd figured she could have a quick coffee and be in a cab by 7:30 and, assuming there would be morning traffic, arrive at the airport before 9.

Wiping the sleep from her eyes, she turned to the window and pulled up her email. She saw the subject line a second before she looked up.

ARLANDA SHUT DOWN DUE TO STORM

Lifting her eyes to the glass, her mouth dropped open. The snow was piled high on the balcony, probably two feet deep, and it wasn't letting up. Reaching for the remote, Remi put the TV onto the lowest volume and searched for the weather.

Of course, she couldn't understand what they were saying, but the pictures were enough. The whole city was blanketed in white.

"The worst in decades," Mats yawned from behind.

Remi turned and furrowed her brow in question.

"That's what it says up there. We haven't had snowfall like this in over twenty years."

He stretched and went to the kitchen. "Coffee?"

Unsure of what to do, Remi stayed quiet. According to her email, all flights leaving Arlanda had been canceled until further notice. So she wasn't leaving Stockholm any time soon.

"Remi?" he called. "Coffee?"

She opened her mouth to respond just as her phone buzzed. Nodding to Mats, she slid her finger across the screen and let out a sharp breath.

"You see the news, Boss?" Chris sounded tired but not disappointed.

"Looking now. Though the window was enough."

"Yeah," he sighed. "I guess we're stuck here, huh?"

"Looks like it. You guys OK at the hotel?" she asked, running a hand through her hair.

"*Oh...*" he sang down the line. "So you're *not* at the hotel. Good for you, Cap. Much better way to spend your downtime than sitting around watching Swedish TV."

Remi rolled her eyes. "Yeah, yeah. Just keep your phone charged. The snow should stop soon, and we'll probably be called back in last-minute."

"Not a chance!" Mats called from the kitchen.

"What he say?" Chris asked, chuckling.

"Ignore him. Charge your phone. Stay warm." She hung up before he could say anything else and tossed her phone on the couch.

Mats came over with two coffees. He handed her one and leaned in for a kiss, his lips gentle against hers as his tongue briefly made contact. Remi put her free hand on his cheek and pulled him closer.

The way he made her feel was crazy. As soon as he got close enough to touch it was like she lost all control. Yes, he was sexy from afar, and she loved watching him move. But the second he put his hands on her, she had an overwhelming desire to rip his clothes off.

"Good morning," he murmured when she finally let him go.

"Good morning." Remi smiled, lifting the coffee to her lips. "Thanks."

"Are you hungry?" he asked, turning on his heel and making his way into the kitchen again.

"After last night, how could I not be?"

Remi walked up to the counter and leaned her arms on the cold stone. He picked up his phone, and music started playing from a speaker she couldn't see. Remi enjoyed her coffee while Mats confidently pulled food from the fridge and turned the stove on.

He whisked eggs and fried bacon, sipping his coffee every few minutes before flashing her a smile. Again, she thought about what it would be like to wake up to this every day. Him cooking for her. Spending lazy weekends on the couch with a book.

Fucking like crazy whenever the urge hit. It felt good.

"More coffee?" he asked, bringing her back to reality.

Remi held her cup out and took a seat on the stool. Mats served her a plate full of creamy scrambled eggs with scallions, bacon, and cheese. He also put out a platter with fresh bread and a selection of meats and cheeses.

"You guys take breakfast this seriously every day?" she joked, scooping some eggs onto her fork.

"When we have time," he chuckled, coming to sit beside her.

"Well, this is amazing. Thank you."

"Tack," he offered.

Thanks.

"Tack," she echoed, grabbing some bread.

They ate quietly, enjoying the music and each other's company. When they were both stuffed, Mats dutifully did the dishes, insisting she relax on the couch.

"I feel bad," Remi said sarcastically, moving quickly and falling into the plush sofa.

"You're my guest. It's my pleasure."

Remi pursed her lips as she watched him in from across the big open room. She'd never had a guy make her more than a coffee, so seeing this tall, gorgeous man move confidently around the kitchen was such a turn-on.

How was he doing it? How was it possible that she was so affected by him? She'd felt it almost immediately - the second the pair made eye contact at the bar. He'd smiled at her, and she'd felt a flutter in her stomach. She'd wanted him right away, and the more they'd talked, the wetter she'd become.

In all her years, she'd never gone to bed with a guy so fast. They almost always had to work for it, be it dinner, drinks, or at the very least, a little conversation.

But Mats? He'd had her at, *Hey, can I get a Kronenbourg, please?*

"What are you thinking?" he called from the kitchen as he loaded the dishwasher.

"I'm trying to figure out what's wrong with you," she explained, leaning back on her elbows and crossing her ankles.

"Wrong with me?"

"Yeah, you have to have something? You can't tell me you're this sexy all the time. I mean, you cook, you fuck, and you're pretty easy to look at. So...where's your issue? You got a wife and kids? An ex that's gonna show up and try to kill me?"

Mats laughed and shrugged. "I can't just be a nice guy?"

She shook her head. "I don't know. I've never met one before." Remi sat up and proceeded to the front door. She opened a drawer on the side table and quipped, "Where do you keep your dirty little secrets?"

"In the bedroom closet, of course," he replied with a serious tone and a smile. "Where else?"

Remi looked at his face and couldn't figure out if he was playing.

"You want to see?" he proposed after a minute of silence.

"I don't know...do it?"

He took her hand and pulled her to the bedroom. She sat on the bed as he ducked into the closet and lifted a box from the corner. It was black with gold trim, and he sat it on the bed between them.

"Go ahead. Take a look."

Remi hesitated, nervous about what she'd find. But when she lifted the lid, her eyes lit up.

Inside the box was an array of sex toys. She lifted out handcuffs and dildos and app-controlled vibrators. He had all kinds of lubes and even a piece of lingerie not unlike what she'd worn the last time she'd been with Sébastien.

"Are you still worried?" he mused, trying to gauge her reaction.

She smiled and raised an eyebrow. "So...you're like, Mr. Grey or something?"

"Haha." He grinned and shrugged his shoulders. "Hardly. I just like to play sometimes. I've found many women appreciate a man who is willing to incorporate this stuff in the bedroom. And-" he stopped and started shuffling through the box. Finally, he found what he was looking for and held it out so she could see. "I'm an investor."

She took the small black box and read the gold words: *Sluta inte!* There was a little card attached with more Swedish she didn't understand.

Inside she found what looked like a strap-on dildo, but it had two thick, steel rings on the end.

"What does it mean?" she wondered aloud, running her hand over the silky gold letters.

"Don't stop," Mats replied. "My friend started the shop about ten years ago and asked me for a loan. When he became successful, rather than just paying me back, I became a partner of sorts. So, I get sent a lot of new and fun things to try."

"And this?" Remi lifted the black dildo from the box, feeling its weight.

"I haven't tried that one yet. And anything in here is cleaned and sanitized, in case you were wondering."

She stayed quiet for a few minutes, putting the black strap on away and lifting different toys from the box, trying to figure out what each did. She'd never been super into toys since she was never afraid to ask for what she wanted. But the few times she had tried it, she'd had a lot of fun.

"Are you turned off by all this?" Mats challenged, his eyes searching her face. "Because it's not something I need. Obviously, I'm just as thrilled to be with you without any extras."

Choosing her words carefully, Remi plucked a bottle of lube from the box. It was whipped cream flavor.

"I'm willing to try anything once." She lifted her eyes to his and added, "With the right partner."

Mats smiled and let out a small, relieved breath. "Most of what's in there is pretty beginner-friendly. No dominant stuff and no real need for safe words."

He picked out a small pink silicone toy. It was curved like a horseshoe; only one end was wider than the other. "This goes inside you," he whispered, touching the wider end. "And this goes on your clit. It's got a few vibration settings, and I can control it with my phone. So it's something you can use in bed... or out at dinner, for example."

Remi took it and flicked the switch, the vibrations feeling good against her fingertips. She turned the toy off and found another. It was glass and very long, at least seven inches. Made up of large beads, the top end was tapered slightly, while the bottom was much more prominent. Though she already knew where this went, she asked anyway.

"What do you do with this?"

He took it from her and put a finger on the end. "I put plenty of lube right here, and then, once you're relaxed and ready, I gently guide it into your perfect ass."

Remi could feel herself getting turned on. Looking at these toys and knowing the pleasure he could bring her with them made her groin warm up. She shifted on the bed and picked up the small box again. She didn't actually know what the thing did.

"And this?"

Mats lifted the toy and touched one of the steel rings. "These are for me. They go on my cock and balls, and then this," he said, running a hand along the thick, black dildo, "is for you."

She furrowed her brow and thought about it for a second. "For me? But...you'd be wearing it so how-" She cut herself short once she got it. "So, this is for... *double* penetration?"

Mats nodded and put it back in the box. "Maybe not the most beginner-friendly."

"It wouldn't be my first time with anal. But I've never…" Her voice trailed off. Remi could feel her need for him getting stronger, and looking at all the toys; she couldn't imagine *not* trying one. "Which is your favorite?"

TWENTY-TWO

Mats blew out a breath and looked down at the box. He chewed the inside of his cheek a little, hovering his hand over the toys as he tried to decide. After a couple of minutes, he pulled a small satin bag from the bottom along with what looked like a cock ring.

"This would be for us both," he whispered, showing her the dual rings. His finger pressed a tiny nub, turning on the small bullet vibe that would inevitably wind up on her clit. "These go around me, holding it in place. And these little bumps," he added, bringing it into her hand and running them over her fingers. "They're for you. They work well without the vibe, too."

Turning the vibe off, he left the ring in her hand and lifted another little bag from the box. He kept his eyes on hers while he undid the small knot and pulled out what looked like two large tweezers.

They were rose gold with a small pearl hanging off the curved end. From there, it split in two, leading up to black nubs. He moved the small piece connecting the pincers, closing the ends until they touched.

"These are nipple clamps. If you've never used them, I have a feeling they will soon be something you'll beg for."

Remi smirked and took one in her hand. She put the black silicone over her pinky finger and moved the center piece up until it pinched. It hurt a little but sent a jolt of pleasure to her clit. She'd always loved it when guys tugged and sucked on her nipples, so this seemed like a no-brainer.

"Remi," Mats began, taking the toys from her and putting his hands in hers. He squeezed and sighed, "We don't have to use any toys. Like I said before, this isn't something that I-"

"I want to."

He put a hand to her cheek and searched her eyes. "Don't say that if you're unsure. I don't want you doing anything you're uncomfortable with."

Remi laughed, bowled over at his consideration and apparent affection.

"I'm sure. In fact, I'm more torn over what to choose first," she whispered, taking the cock ring back in her hands. "I like the idea of slipping this on you. And these bumps would probably feel pretty good."

Mats brought his leg onto the bed and turned to face her. He pushed the box aside and reached for her thigh. With his other hand, he tried to move the box with the double penetration strap on, but she stopped him. Then, placing her hand over his, she cleared her throat.

"You got anything…smaller. To start out with?"

"Hmmm," he pondered, reaching to the big box again, coming back to her with something that looked more like a decorative paperweight.

It was pink, and glass, with an intricate rose on one end and a tapered bulb on the other. It was much smaller than the other glass dildo she'd looked at.

"This is pretty discreet, but you'll definitely feel it when I fuck you."

His words made her breath catch.

"Fuck, Mats," she breathed, looking between the toys and wondering if she would even last long enough to try them all.

Reading her mind, he closed the gap and kissed her. She had the cock ring in one hand and the glass butt plug in the other. The thought of him using them on her was so fucking sexy, but given how her body reacted to him, she worried that she'd cum way too soon.

Mats pulled away when he felt her drawing him closer. He left the cock ring and butt plug with Remi, lifted a bottle of lube out, and then put the box away. The nipple clamps were still in his hand when he turned back, purposefully taking his sweater off, his eyes searing into hers with nothing but lust.

"We're going to take this slowly, OK? You're gonna beg me to hurry, but I want you to feel everything I'm going to do to you, got it?"

She nodded and stood, putting the toys on the bed as she quickly removed her sweater.

"I should...uh...use the bathroom." She blushed and hurried to the door.

He grabbed her wrist. "Check the cupboard in the corner. Bottom shelf."

Leaving him in the bedroom was tough, especially

when every step she took made her clit throb. But if they were going to be using that glass plug, she had to prepare.

In the cupboard, she found what she was looking for, opting to use the shower so she'd be as clean as possible for him. When she was done, she wrapped herself in a towel and tiptoed back to the bedroom. He was on the bed, shirt and pants off, his dark blue briefs tight and inviting.

"Come," he ordered, holding his hand out to her.

She did as she was told, marching forward until he could just about reach. On the bed, beside him, the clamps and butt plug were laid out in a neat row on the white sheets. Even though he'd obviously decided against using the cock ring, she felt a rush of excitement and moved to take off the towel.

Mats reached and grabbed her hand, stopping her with a dark look. He shook his head and pulled her closer.

"I need you to know that I'm in control here. Of course, I'm here to please you, and I need you to know that I'm not the kind of person that enjoys seeing people in pain. So, if anything hurts or feels uncomfortable, you need to tell me. If you'd feel safer, we can decide on a safe word."

His sudden serious tone gave her pause, but his oddly sweet words only made her want him even more.

"How about...JFK?" She smiled and raised an eyebrow.

"JFK? OK. If you feel anything other than pleasure,

you tell me to stop, and I'll stop immediately. I promise you that. I'll always stop, OK?"

"Mats. This isn't-"

"*This* isn't overly serious, no. *This* isn't bondage, and you won't be tied up. But it's important to me that you enjoy this."

She felt a wave of emotion at his words and leaned down to kiss him, straddling him as she did, her naked pussy rubbing up against his briefs.

He moved his hand between them and found her slit, running down until he touched her opening.

"You feel ready," he chuckled into her mouth. "I like that."

Suddenly, he lifted her and propped her on her feet. Then, he grabbed at the towel and pulled it down in one swift motion, leaving her naked and vulnerable in front of him.

She wanted to reach for him, to grab his cock and take it in her mouth. But he'd said he was in control, and she'd never wanted to follow orders so badly before.

Mats looked at her, taking her body in greedily, lifting a hand to her breast before trailing down to her slit. He thrust his finger a few times before bringing it back to his mouth, licking her juices with a sigh. Then he looked to his side and muttered, "Where to begin."

TWENTY-THREE

Standing in front of Mats, totally exposed in the middle of the day, Remi felt nothing but desire. She didn't feel self-conscious or embarrassed - she felt empowered and excited. He did that to her with just a look.

"We'll start with these, OK?" Mats announced after a minute, grabbing the nipple clamps and holding them up to her.

She nodded enthusiastically, keeping still as he reached for her hips. He pulled her close until her knees touched the bed between his legs. With a deep sigh, he ran his hands over her breasts, worshipping them with his fingers until he leaned forward and took her right nipple in his mouth.

Remi moaned as his tongue swirled around, moving to her other side seconds later. He sucked and licked for what felt like hours, then slipped his fingers between her legs.

The sudden invasion made her jolt with pleasure, and she had to put her hand on his shoulder. He worked her slowly, sucking, tugging, and stroking her nerves until he heard her breath hitch.

When he pulled his hands and mouth free, she

whimpered, opening her eyes to see him lift the clamps. He locked eyes with her for approval, and she greedily gave it to him.

Mats put his whole focus on her right nipple, which was hard and already sensitive. He took it in his mouth again, gently rolling his tongue across and around before pulling away and placing the black silicone nubs at the base. As he slid the center piece up, she felt it tighten.

"How's that?" he asked before taking it any further.

"Mmmmm. It feels good."

Mats took that as a confirmation to keep going and lifted the metal further until it pinched enough to stay in place. Then he moved to the other side, repeating the process of sucking and licking before gently slipping the clamp in position.

When he let go, they stayed put, and the gentle pinching felt amazing. Then he reached up and tugged on one, sending a pulse straight to her clit. Reading her body, Mats very tenderly licked at her nipples and slipped his fingers back between her legs, pulling gently on the tiny pearls as he worked her into a frenzy.

His excruciatingly slow pace was driving her crazy, but she knew that she had to wait. They were only just getting started.

He stood abruptly, taking her head in his free hand as he kissed her deeply and with urgency. His other hand was still between her legs, but he trailed the other down, plucking at the clamp. It hurt, but in a good way, and she gasped as he did it again with the other.

"Are you ready for more?" he whispered, leaning his forehead against hers.

"God, yes."

"Get on the bed. On your knees," he growled, moving to one side so she could get by.

As she had the day before, Remi climbed onto the bed with her ass in the air, and she swayed a little, inviting him in. He didn't need much encouragement, and before she had the chance to steady herself, he was behind her, his lips on her pussy and his tongue inside.

"Oh, *fuck*! Fuck, Mats!" Remi cried out, gripping at the sheets.

His hand found her breast and tugged again, causing her to arch her back. His other hand found her hips to keep her steady while he licked her sex and found her clit.

She felt his knees come on the bed, and he pushed her forward. Remi obeyed, twisting turned back to see him lift the butt plug. She clenched at the sight of it, but her heart raced in anticipation.

"I'm going to be very gentle. If it hurts, you stop me." It wasn't a question, and his tone was back to serious.

"I'm ready," Remi breathed, pushing her hips back, so he had better access.

The lube was cold at first, but then his hands were on her, warming and comforting. She felt what could only be his thumb at her back entrance and took a deep breath. Deftly, he reached his fingers to her clit, working her front and back until she relaxed, groaning into the sheets.

When he removed his thumb, she wanted to tense, but he pressed her harder, working her nub in slow and steady strokes. Then she felt the cool end of the plug rubbing from her pussy to her ass. After a few passes, he stayed put, pressing gently at her opening.

He stayed there for a minute, allowing her to get a feel for the glass. Then he slipped it inside, her tight ass opening to accept it a lot faster than she'd imagined. His other hand left her clit, and she heard him add more lube as he pulled the plug back, fucking her ass with just the top couple of inches.

True to his words, Mats took it slow. He gave her the tip only, reaching around once more and stroking at her clit to help her along. Gradually, he added more length, and she felt herself expanding.

"Oh! Shit," Remi gasped when the whole thing was finally in place. "Oh god. That feels amazing."

Behind her, she heard him chuckle as he took hold of the flower and tugged. Remi fell forward, the sensation tipping her to breaking point.

"Not yet," he said, letting go, leaving the glass plug in place.

Peering over her shoulder, she saw him looking at her. His eyes were heavy and full of need. She felt his hands on her again, trailing over her ass until one slid down and around to her aching sex, while the other reached her tits. She'd almost forgotten about the clamps until he tugged at them again. This time she felt a new kind of pleasure mixed with the nerve in her ass as she clenched.

"Come here," he whispered, putting his hand on her arm.

She turned and lifted her body up, the plug moving as she did. For a second, she worried it would get lost, but then she felt the glass rose. It wasn't going anywhere.

Finally, Mats stood and took off his briefs. His big, hard dick popped free, and she couldn't help but let out a moan of appreciation.

"Oh, wow."

He'd already put the cock ring in place, and now that his dick was swollen, it sat snuggly at the base. Remi couldn't help herself and had the tip in her mouth before he could stop her. If he wanted to, he didn't. Instead, he put his hand on her head and groaned as she worked him, swirling and sucking.

She was on her knees, and with every bob, she felt the plug. He reached out and twisted the left clamp, just an inch or so. But it was enough. She let his dick fall free as she cried his name aloud.

When she could think again, she devoured his thick, beautiful cock, greedily sucking and licking as it swelled in her mouth.

After a few minutes, he seemed to gain his control and pulled her back. Then, he lifted her until she was upright on her knees and brought his hands to her nipples.

"How do these feel?" he asked with a slight pull on them both.

"Oh! *Fuck*, they feel good."

"I'm going to tighten them now." He did it quickly, slipping the divider up another inch until she gasped.

The pain swelled and passed until all she felt was pleasure. Her pussy ached, and her clit was begging for release. She smiled and reached out to him, but he shook his head and lifted his hand, twirling his finger in the air.

"I'm going to fuck you on your knees."

The words made her stomach clench, which made the butt plug twitch, and the intake of breath made the clamps pinch. She felt agony and satisfaction across her whole body. It was on the verge of overwhelming, but she still wanted more.

Following his orders, Remi turned until she was on all fours again. Gripping the sheets, she tensed, waiting for him to finally give her what she wanted.

Mats moved in slowly, his dick sliding from her soaking pussy to her clit. Then he slipped inside, just a couple of inches to give her the time to get used to it.

She'd never felt anything like it before, and the feeling was intense. Being penetrated in her ass and her pussy was as full as she'd ever been, and she hesitated for a second, worried his whole length would be too much.

Still, when he asked if she wanted more, she heard herself groan "yes." So mats gave it to her, thrusting his long hard dick all the way inside, filling her from front to back and drawing a cry of pleasure from her lips.

When he pulled back, she could feel his dick running against the bulb in her ass, touching nerve endings she didn't know were there. He slammed into her again and again, and she could hear he was starting to breathe heavily too.

As he pulled himself free, Remi felt a sudden emptiness. She turned back, ready to question him, but he had her rolling onto her back before she could speak.

Mats tugged at her right breast, and she heard him click the bullet vibrator on. He was back inside in seconds, pounding into her harder and faster, the buzzing sending pleasure over her entire sex.

After a couple dozen pussy splitting thrusts, Mats started to slow. He came down onto her and licked at her nipple, positioning himself, so the bullet was right on her clit. He moved slowly, grinding it in place and watching her eyes widen.

He could see she was close and tugged her left nipple clamp off, taking it in his mouth as she whimpered. He ground into her further, the vibrations too much and not enough all at the same time.

Finally, when he pulled the other clamp free, Remi called his name, her orgasm hitting like a freight train. It was as intense as she'd ever felt until he reached down and tugged at the butt plug.

Somehow, as he pulled it free, she came again. Her body contracted and twitched as she was overwhelmed with pleasure and pain. Her nipples throbbed, her pussy ached, and the buzzing on her clit brought her close to breaking point.

Luckily, he was right behind her. He came in a

rushing groan, grunting her name as he hit his peak, thrusting the last of him into her before he slumped and pulled himself free.

Remi heard the bullet turn off and thought she heard him speak, but her ears were ringing, and her head was fuzzy. Her heart was pounding, and it felt like every nerve ending in her body was on fire.

"Remi?" he asked again, trying to catch his breath. "Was it good for you?"

Licking her lips and taking a deep breath, Remi couldn't help but laugh.

"I think that was the best sex of my life."

TWENTY-FOUR

They showered together, Mats gently washing her with soap. He moved expertly, avoiding her nipples and clit, knowing they would be sensitive still. When he wrapped her in a towel, she nestled into him, resting her head on his chest.

He kissed her head and held her, breathing in the steam for a few minutes. Eventually, it started to dissipate and turn chilly, so they both got dressed and opted to put on a movie.

"You feeling hungry?" Mats asked as Remi navigated to Netflix.

"Always."

"I know a great place that delivers sushi, but I'm guessing that's not an option today."

Realizing she'd essentially forgotten about the snow, Remi turned to the window. To her shock, it was still coming down, though not as heavy.

"How about sandwiches?" Mats offered, his head in the fridge.

"I'm happy with anything," Remi called.

She clicked through the titles as he opened packages and clinked silverware. Eventually, he came to sit beside her, two plates loaded with open-faced sandwiches and a big bag of chips in his teeth.

"This looks amazing!" she cried, taking in the food.

They each had two pieces of soft seeded bread, covered with meats and cheese, plus some kind of creamy spread and a few red onions on top. It looked like it came from a cafe, and Remi sighed at how perfect it all was.

She closed her eyes when she took the first bite, handing the remote over so she could focus on the food. Minutes went by while he navigated the titles. She had to laugh, knowing it could take hours before they found anything.

"What are you in the mood for?" She suggested.

He ran his hand down her thigh and grazed the thin fabric between his thumb and her clit. "I don't think you're ready for what I'm in the mood for."

With a slight pout, Remi kissed him. She leaned close and let his tongue slip into her mouth. Even after mind-blowing sex, just his kiss was enough to get her going.

"How about something scary?"

Mats found something that looked gruesome and started the movie. They ate while the family explored their new house, brushing off the clear signs it was haunted. Remi ate every last bite and most of the chips before letting out a deep breath and sitting back into the couch.

Mats finished not long after and sat back, lifting his arm up and around her shoulders. Remi nestled into the gap, fitting against his chest perfectly, her feet tucked up under her body, her knees resting on his thigh. He lifted his hand to her shoulder and squeezed, resting his head on hers as he pulled a blanket over them both.

Neither moved an inch throughout the movie, and when it finished, Remi shifted her arm around his waist and set her head on his chest.

"It wasn't that bad." Mats laughed.

"No. No, it was fine. I'm just sleepy, I guess."

"Take a nap, if you want. Not like we're going anywhere," he added, gesturing to the window.

"I'm OK. In fact, I'm dying to know more about your friend's little shop. Like, did you know what kind of shop it was before you gave him the money? Were you into all that already, or was it just that you had unlimited access all of a sudden?"

He chuckled, and she sat up to see his reaction.

"I guess, no. I hadn't really tried anything like that before. Not that I was against it - I just hadn't had the opportunity. And yes, I did know what the shop was."

"What was the first toy you tried?" she demanded, raising her eyebrows and nudging him gently in the ribs.

"Um, it was a while ago. I think…it was a small vibrator. Nothing big and crazy. Just discreet. My partner at the time suggested it actually after meeting my friend and hearing about the shop."

"And since then, have you ever…you know…" She trailed off, but he didn't seem to follow her train of thought. "You know! Have *you* ever tried anything… on yourself?"

He dropped his head back and laughed. "I've never

ELIZABETH HARDY

really had that desire, no. I've always been more concerned about my partner's pleasure, and seeing that is what gets me off."

"I've noticed." Remi smiled, biting her lip.

"Have you?" Mats invited, turning the focus onto her. "You told me yesterday you have a few men that you spend time with. What does that mean, exactly?"

Remi had never been shy about her sex life, and she'd never been ashamed of her promiscuity. She was a grown woman who enjoyed sex, and she was sure to have it as often as she could.

But staring into his eyes, she suddenly didn't feel like sharing.

"I just meant that I date a little, here and there."

His eyes narrowed, and he tilted his head. "You don't need to lie, Remi. I'm not going to judge you."

She stirred on the couch, uncomfortable and suddenly warm. "I'm just...I guess you could say I have a few guys in certain cities that I like to visit. It's just about...you know. They're fun, and we have fun, and then I leave."

With her eyes down, she couldn't see his reaction. But she noticed his arm pull back at her words.

"Right," he muttered.

"Mats," Remi said quickly, putting her hand on his arm before he could get up. "Come on. We're having fun, right? This is good, whatever it is. Can't it just stay like that? Can't we just enjoy this?"

"Of course," he replied with a smile she could tell wasn't real. "I'm all about having fun." He moved closer and put his hand on her right breast. "How are

152

you feeling, by the way?" He tightened his grip, and she felt a twinge but no pain.

"Sensitive, but OK," she answered.

"Sensitive, but OK," he echoed, pushing so she fell onto her back.

Mats lifted her shirt and kissed her belly, gliding his tongue up to her breasts. She wasn't wearing a bra, and when his lips touched the edge of her nipple, she gasped. He pulled away, but she put her hand on his head and pressed until he had her in his mouth again.

She felt a little bit of pain but the pleasure far outweighed it. Plus, he kept his touch light. No sucking or tugging, just licking and squeezing with his hand. For a few minutes, Remi was happy to let him play, but when she started to feel that now too familiar ache, she pushed herself up.

Before he had time to stop her, she stood and bent over, pulling her pants and underwear down. Then she pulled her shirt off and nodded her head at him.

"Take your pants off," she ordered, placing her hands on her hips.

As he moved, she turned and had an idea. Deciding it was her turn to give orders, she sauntered past him and took a seat in the armchair. When he went to stand, she held up her hand to stay him.

"Uh uh. You stay right there."

Remi brought her hand to her breasts and squeezed them together, taking her nipples between her fingers to test their sensitivity. She rolled them before pinching, her clit responding with a sharp pulse.

When she opened her eyes, Mats was sitting upright, his eyes on her tits and his hands tapping his thighs. She smirked and put her fingers in her mouth, sucking on them before moving south.

Her pussy wasn't as wet as it had been, but she had no trouble slipping her fingers inside. She moved in and out, trailing back up to her clit with a gasp. With her other hand, she pinched at her nipple, keeping her eyes on Mats the whole time.

"Stand up," she breathed, her fingers moving faster between her legs.

He did as he was told, his dick standing up to attention behind his underwear.

"Take those off."

He did, quickly, kicking them aside. Her eyes widened as he stood upright, never tiring of how much she wanted him.

"Touch yourself," she demanded. "I wanna see you stroking that thing like it's my pussy."

Mats put his big hand around his cock and started to caress himself. She saw his eyes close and pressed her fingers harder, her clit already sensitive and screaming for release.

She rolled lazy circles across her pussy until he opened his eyes again and met her gaze. Remi lifted her now slick finger and beckoned him forward. As he did, she stood and met him in the middle, her hand still on her tit. She offered it to him, and Mats greedily reached down, his mouth hot and wet, sending a wave of pleasure between her legs.

"You're gonna fuck me now. I want it hard and fast.

I want you to slam that big cock into me so hard I have to hold on. Got it?"

It was Mats' turn to bite his lip this time. He nodded and rushed her, wrapping his arms around her back and kissing her with urgency. She felt one hand leave her as the other lifted her off her feet. He moved them into the kitchen, stopping only when her ass hit the island.

She'd barely opened her eyes when dropped to his knees, his tongue on her clit, sucking it between his teeth in seconds. But as good as it felt, she needed to feel him inside her.

"Fuck me, Mats. *Hard*!"

He stood, bringing a couch pillow with him, and turned her around. In a moment of sweetness, he put the pillow in between her hips and the granite. Then he bent her over and positioned his cock at her opening. She felt his fingers lubricate her pussy, and then he was inside.

As promised, he rammed into her, making her thankful for the cushion. He wasn't gentle. Mats put his hand in her hair and pulled until her back was arched. She clutched at the counter as he hammered into her, over and over, the pressure building inside.

He was moving too hard and too fast to let go and touch her, and he was too far gone to slow down. Mats came with a groan minutes later, twitching inside as he fell into her back. But even in his spent state, he wasn't done. He spun her around and put his hand on her pussy.

Using his own juices, he roughly stroked her clit

with his knuckles, taking her nipple in his mouth. She fell back, arched on her shoulders as he worked her with his hands. They were everywhere, inside and on her clit all at once, and she could feel she was close.

Remi started to gasp, moaning as he finger fucked her on the counter. Then he moved to one side and pulled his fingers free. Using the new angle, he opened her legs wide he started spanking her. Light taps at first and then stronger and faster. It was enough to send her over the edge, and as she shouted out his name, he thrust his fingers back inside, stroking her G-spot to keep her orgasm rolling.

When she finally came down, he was standing over her, his beautiful glistening dick on her thigh and his eyes happy and tired. She stood and put her hand on his chest. He put his own over hers and tightened his hold.

Remi felt a different kind of flutter in her stomach this time. Ignoring it, she smiled, tapped his ass, and strutted to the bathroom once more.

"I think I'm gonna owe you for your next water bill," she joked.

Mats laughed but stayed put, choosing not to join her this time.

TWENTY-FIVE

After showering himself, Mats made his way back into the kitchen. He rooted around in the freezer, moving a few things into the fridge for later before offering Remi a tea.

"Sure," she shrugged, standing by the window, watching the snowfall.

As Mats shuffled around behind her, Remi grabbed her phone to check the weather. The snow wasn't letting up, though it wasn't as crazy as the day before. Still, she doubted anyone would be flying today.

"Here," Mats offered, coming to stand at her side. He glanced at her phone and asked, "Anything?"

Remi scrolled into her emails, finding a new one from the airline.

"No flights today." She sighed.

They stood by the window, quietly drinking their tea and watching the grey skies.

Unsure of how she felt, Remi wished she could read his mind. Was he happy about the cancellations, or did that just make things more complicated? This was supposed to be a one-time thing, and now they were practically living together. Yes, it had only been a day, but with Mats, it felt like longer.

She felt like she knew him already. As though they'd connected somehow, and this was...what? Not love. Right?

Don't be a fucking moron, she thought, closing her eyes. *Yes, he's gorgeous and sexy and smart and sweet and fucking perfect. Yes, you want to jump his bones every time he smiles at you, and yes, you've never orgasmed like you do with him before. But what? What do you expect after a day? Jesus Christ, Remi. Get it together.*

"Hey, you OK?" Mats nudged her with his elbow.

She kept her eyes on her tea and nodded. "Yeah. Just wondering if this snow will ever end."

"Would it be so bad if it didn't?" he muttered into his drink.

Remi glanced his way, his eyes refusing to meet hers. "I don't know."

After a few minutes of silence, Mats put his cup down and clapped his hands together. "Feel like a walk?"

"In this?" Remi questioned.

"Why not? It's letting up, and you won't believe how quiet the city is in the snow."

Somehow, he convinced her, grabbing plenty of layers and an extra thick jacket. It basically drowned her, but she felt warm and secure. Before long, they were pushing their way out the side door and into the hip-high powder. Her hip, of course.

Mats was right, though; the city was eerily quiet. They trudged their way towards the water, and Mats brushed the snow off a bench. How he found it, she didn't know, but she couldn't help but laugh at how crazy they must've looked.

"You were right," Remi admitted after a few minutes. "It is letting up."

They passed a few other brave souls as they progressed further down the river and heard some kids having a blast near the park. When Remi tripped, Mats caught her arm and chuckled.

"Careful, babe."

Babe?

For some reason, the word made Remi panic. She pulled her arm back and turned, not wanting him to see the look on her face. But she couldn't see the curb beneath the snow and fell, landing in the middle of the powder.

When Mats came to get her, he tripped on the same curb but managed to catch himself on a street sign.

It wobbled above her, shaking snow onto her face. She gasped at the cold and laughed out loud, looking up to see Mats. He was gorgeous and fun and looked at her with kind yet lustful eyes.

She reached up and tugged him down, snickering at the grunt he let out when he landed on her. Before he could say anything, she kissed him. Her gloved hand found his cheek, and she rolled on top, pushing her tongue into his mouth and moaning at how right it felt.

As if on cue, some of the snow fell on her back, and she arched up, crying out as the cold made its way into her jacket.

"Fuck, that's cold!"

Mats grinned and helped her up, brushing the

snow from her hair and away from her neck.

"Maybe that's enough outside time today, huh?"

Remi nodded and took his outstretched hand. Then, realizing she had no clue which way to go, she snuggled close, tucking her arm around his as he guided her through the powder once more.

Back at his apartment, they shed their snow-covered clothes and boots, shivering as it turned to water and dripped onto their skin.

"I'll get some towels," Mats promised, hustling into the bathroom.

When her phone rang, Remi hesitated. Did she want to hear what the airline had to say?

Knowing they would just keep calling, she hurried to the window and swiped to answer the call. Choosing to keep her reaction private, she opened the door to the balcony and stepped outside.

"Scott."

"Captain Scott, hi. We're calling to let you know that Arlanda is still closed. But the snow is letting up, and it looks like you'll be seeing it warm up. They're confident things will be back up and running tomorrow, so keep your phone close by, OK?"

"Yeah, sure," Remi mumbled, dropping her hand as the agent hung up.

Before she had time to process, Mats was at her back.

"What are you doing? You're gonna get sick." He wrapped a towel around her shoulders and started to rub her arms.

Remi stayed still, chewing on her cheek as she

thought about another day in Stockholm. Another day with Mats. She couldn't deny that she was happy to hear the news, but she also felt something else - something she couldn't quite put her finger on.

"Was that the airline?" Mats asked, breaking her out of her daze.

"Oh, uh, yeah," she replied, spinning to face him. "Looks like we'll be flying out tomorrow."

She watched his face, trying to gauge his reaction. Luckily, he didn't hide anything and grinned, reaching down and lifting her into a kiss.

Whatever that other thing she'd been feeling was melted away, and she clutched him closer, lifting her legs around his waist. When he put her down, he held her face in his hands and smiled and let out a short breath of contentment before kissing her again. Remi got as close as she could and slipped her hands under his shirt. She traced them over his toned abs and hard chest, feeling her way around his strong shoulders.

Mats responded by sliding his hand under her shirt. She gasped at how cold it was but let out a small moan when he reached her breast. Kissing her again, Mats pinched and rolled her nipple in his fingers before breaking free from her lips, yanking her shirt up and taking her in his mouth.

Not wanting to waste a second, Remi shimmied out of her pants and underwear, the snow on the table behind her causing her to jump when she made contact.

In a rush, she reached for him, pulling his sweats and underwear down to his ankles. His mouth returned to her nipple as she put her fingers in her mouth, licking at them until they were wet and warm.

She tugged him backward until her ass was perched on the freezing table. With one hand on his chest, Remi pushed him back, sliding the other, wet fingers into her sex. She worked herself for a few seconds before clutching his shirt and yanking him into her.

Mats didn't waste a second, grabbing his already swelling cock and finding her opening. The instant they touched and the head of his dick pushed its way inside, they both let out a groan of desire. Her eyes closed, Remi held onto his shoulder as he thrust in and out. They shot open when she felt the chill on her breasts.

Mats used the snow, gently rubbing it over her tits until he saw goosebumps on her flesh. Then he stroked and sucked until they were pink, and she was gasping for more.

Using the same cold piece of snow, Mats locked his eyes on hers and thrust his hand between her legs. The rough snow soon melted against her throbbing slit, leaving his wet fingers behind.

Not once did he stop his pounding into her, and she could feel his cock swelling the closer he got. Taking advantage of the angle they were at, she lifted forward and took his nipple in her mouth, biting at it and drawing a groan of satisfaction and pain from his lips. His fingers slipped free as he grabbed at the table for support.

Soon enough, one hand was in her hair, pulling her

head back, so he had full access to her neck.

The table started to move as he pushed harder. Remi reached down and touched herself, rubbing her fingers roughly across her clit, her eyes now focussed on his thick cock. The feeling of him inside brought her closer and closer until he put his hand on hers, stopping the movement for a split second before taking over.

Again, he started to tap at her clit, increasing the pressure until she could hear skin on skin slapping. Somehow, he managed to bend low enough to suck her nipple into his mouth.

Three strokes later, Remi came in a roar of pleasure. He smacked at her and bit her breast as she shuddered and moaned and twitched against him. But he didn't stop. He kept his mouth on her and his fingers firmly on her clit, pressing it with small movements as he pounded harder and harder.

Remi came again, her clit sensitive and begging for release. Her ass involuntarily hitched back as her stomach rolled, and the orgasm came in waves. Then just as quickly, Mats let out a grunt.

"*Fuck!*" he shouted so loud she was sure the neighbors would hear.

He jerked a few more times, his hands now on the table at her sides. When Remi finally stood, she laughed at the impression her ass had left in the snow.

"That was fun," she murmured, stretching up for a kiss.

Mats pulled the towel back around her shoulders and tugged her inside, closing the door behind them.

"It was cold. But yes, fun too."

Remi started to shiver and found herself yet again in the shower. It wasn't long before Mats was at her back. He reached around her waist and rested his hands on her hips, his head on hers as they let the water warm them from the outside in.

"What are you doing to me, Remi?" he whispered into her ear.

That was all it took for her to get that feeling again. The one she couldn't put her finger on. It started to gnaw at her insides as he squeezed her tighter. From out of nowhere, she had an overwhelming desire to run.

Spinning to face him, she wanted to say something funny, or smart, or maybe even a little hurtful. But the second her eyes met his, all she could do was reach up and kiss him.

TWENTY-SIX

Mats made them a delicious dinner, and they both read for a couple of hours before landing in bed. They kissed and touched some but ended up entangled in limbs and falling asleep early.

When Remi woke up the next day, Mats was gone, his side of the bed cold and empty. She rolled over and gave herself time to listen, not hearing anything from the other room.

Eventually, she dragged herself out of bed, throwing on one of his sweaters and her yoga pants before padding into the bathroom. She peed and splashed a little cold water on her face before fixing her hair and going out to say good morning.

But the room was empty. She glanced to the balcony, happy to see the snow had finally stopped and the sun was out. But where was Mats?

She found her phone on the side table and tapped the screen, seeing a text from Susanna from just twenty minutes ago. Figuring she'd still be awake, Remi flopped onto the couch and hit dial. Susanna answered after four rings.

"Remi, it's like, 2 am."

"You texted me, like, 15 minutes ago, Suse!" She

chuckled, grabbing a blanket and pulling it over her feet.

"Yeah, when I got home. Did you even read it?"

Remi shrugged. "I needed to hear it from you, I guess."

Susanna groaned, and Remi could hear her sitting up. She even heard the light flick on as Suse cleared her throat.

"Troy's back in town," she whispered, hesitating for a few seconds.

"Hmmm," Remi replied, not wanting to give her opinion just yet.

After she'd gotten back from Paris, Susanna went out with Troy again. They'd had a great date and even better sex, and he'd called her the next day. They went out a couple more times before he disappeared again. Poof. No more texting. No calls. Just like he had the time before.

Susanna argued that she hadn't wanted anything serious. But Remi could see she was hurt. And now he was back in town, and she was at his beck and call again?

"*Rem*," she hissed. "Don't, OK?"

"Suse, I'm just wondering what his excuse was this time...and what it'll be next time." She heard her friend sigh on the other end and apologized. "Just tell me."

Susanna breathed out and started to dish. "He called me and apologized. He said it was last-minute and he didn't have time to call me. Whatever, right? I don't give a shit. I told him no way he couldn't find a single second to text me after he left, right? So, thanks but no thanks."

Filled with pride, Remi let out a quiet 'woo-hoo.'

"But," Susanna continued. "I left my mom's watch at his place."

"Oh shit."

"Yeah, so I told him I wanted it back and could I come get it. He said yes, and I went by the next day."

"Oh, Suse-"

"He wasn't there! Relax."

Remi groaned and closed her eyes. "Phew."

"But his roommate was…" Susanna murmured.

Remi could picture the smile on her face and the glint in her eyes. She knew her well enough to know that tone.

"Please tell me you fucked him?"

"Oh yeah. Big time. *Remi*! I couldn't help myself. He's beautiful and was so flirty, and when he showed me into Troy's room to find the watch, he flopped onto the bed, just watching me."

"Very hot." Remi giggled.

"Right? So I looked around and found it, and I was so happy because I thought I'd lost it. And then he gets up and comes in close and…I don't know. I just kissed him."

"Damn, girl!"

Susanna laughed. "I let out my inner Remi, I guess."

To her side, the front door opened, and Mats came in, coffees in one hand and a bag full of what she hoped were pastries in the other. He smiled at her and lifted his hands, creeping to the kitchen as he shook off the cold.

"Remi? You still there?"

"Uh...yeah. Hang on," she muttered, dropping her phone so she could speak to Mats. "I just need a sec, OK?"

He nodded and waved her off, grabbing plates and napkins. Remi left him to it and went back into the bedroom. She plopped onto the bed and brought the phone back up to her ear.

"OK, sorry, I-" she began, but Susanna cut her off.

"Are you still with that guy?"

Remi rolled her eyes and nodded. "Kinda."

"Kinda? You texted me yesterday to say you were gonna hit it and get out. How are you still there?"

"The *snow*, Suse. I got stuck!"

"Stuck on his cock." Suse snickered.

"Very funny. It's not...it's just..." but she couldn't lie.

"Rem?"

Remi took a deep breath and blew it out before responding. "I think I'm in trouble, Suse."

"Trouble like he's got you chained to a bedpost. Or trouble like...he's making you rethink your whole life?"

When she didn't reply, Susanna's tone changed. "Wait, I was kidding. But are you telling me you're in *trouble* trouble? Like, you have feelings for this guy? Remi, you've only known him-"

"I know that, Suse! I'm well aware, thanks. But I just...*fuck*. I can't help myself around him, and he's got me thinking that maybe...shit, I don't know."

"Sounds like you're falling for this guy. His cock that good?"

"His cock *is* perfect. His ass is perfect. So's his face and smile, and his eyes, and his fingers, and he cooks, and he's sweet. And every time I look at him, I just want to rip his clothes off and fuck him. But not just fuck him. I want to touch him and kiss him and...just be close to him."

"Fuck me, Remi."

"Yeah. Fuck me." She breathed out, flopping on her back and closing her eyes.

"Well, I mean, that's amazing, babe. I'm so happy for you. You can't just keep- *shhh*."

Remi could hear someone else on the other end and furrowed her brow.

"Uh, Suse. Are you not alone?"

"Um, not...exactly," Susanna admitted with a giggle.

"Hey, Remi!" a voice sang through the phone.

"Who the fuck is that? Is that the roommate?"

"The name's Bryan. Nice to meet you." His deep voice echoed down the line, and she heard her friend squeal.

"You too, Bryan. Shit. Sorry. I hope you were both sleeping, and she didn't answer mid-thrust."

"Nice, Remi."

They both spoke at the same time and laughed, and she had an image of them in bed, him tickling her while she tried to keep a straight face. Suddenly, she felt like a third wheel.

"Ok, love birds. I gotta go. But hey, since you're both up...why not make the most?"

Bryan agreed enthusiastically, and judging from her reply; he already had his hands on Susanna. The pair hung up, and Remi sat, happy for her friend but suddenly nervous to go out and face Mats.

TWENTY-SEVEN

"Hey." Mats grinned when she came out of his room. "I have a bunch of food here." He held up a wooden platter loaded with pastries. "And coffee, of course."

Remi joined him on the couch and opened her mouth to express her delight. But he captured her mouth with his and kissed her like he hadn't seen her in weeks. Unable to control herself, she dissolved into him, her hand on his chest as her heart started to beat faster.

"Good morning," he whispered when they finally pulled apart. "I figured you'd be sick of the bread and meat. The place down the block is open, so I figured, why not?"

"You didn't have to," Remi gushed, her eyes locking on something that looked salty and covered in bacon.

They each ate a pastry and finished half of their coffees before Mats asked, "Was that the airline before?"

"Oh, uh. No. It wasn't. It was my friend Suse."

"Late in New York, no?"

She laughed and nodded. "Yeah. I woke her- *them* up."

"I thought you said she was single?" Mats queried, reaching for a knife and cutting one of the chocolate pastries in half.

"Yeah, she was. I don't know. I guess she met some guy. They sounded cute on the phone."

"Good for her."

Remi gazed at him and knew he was being sincere. It wasn't some throwaway comment - he meant what he said. He'd remembered what she'd told him about Susanna, and he hadn't needed any prompting. He listened when she talked, and he took in what she said.

"We'll see, I guess."

"And, uh, did you get any emails?" His eyes stayed on the food. "I just ask because it's pretty cold outside. Kind of icy, actually."

Picking up her phone, Remi checked her emails first before moving to the weather.

"No emails yet, but you're right. The temperature is dropping."

"Huh," he mused, finishing his coffee and hopping up. "I have a pot on if you want more?"

She nodded and watched him go, draining her own cup and happily accepting the one he came back with. They finished as much of the food as they could before sitting back, his arm around her shoulder as he flicked through the TV.

They watched a home makeover show followed by a show about tiny houses. They chatted, commenting on the homes and design choices, laughing at the crazy colors and ugly tiles.

When he said he'd consider going tiny, Remi roared and leaned over. "You wouldn't even fit in a tiny house!"

"Some of them are tall," he argued, poking a finger into her side, drawing a small cry.

"Come on. You'd spend the rest of our lives ducking your head and complaining that there's no room to move."

Mats lifted his eyes to hers, hearing her words and raising an eyebrow. "The rest of *our* lives?"

She hadn't even heard herself say it. It just slipped out.

Shit. Shit. Shit!

"You know what I mean," she said, waving him off and jumping off the couch.

"Don't do that," he growled, his voice suddenly serious.

"Do what?"

"Run away."

Holding her hands out, she pursed her lips and looked around. "Where am I running?"

Mats groaned and tucked his hands into his lap. He chewed his cheek before looking back at her and asking, "Why do you freak out anytime this gets serious?"

"I...I don't. I mean, this is...this isn't..."

He stood quickly and came forward. She kept her feet in place and looked up at him with confused eyes that even she didn't buy.

"Why are you so hellbent on telling me that this isn't serious? That *this is a one-night thing*? Why can't

173

you let yourself feel this?"

Remi shook her head and shrugged. "Mats, I-"

"You feel this, Remi. I know you do. Whatever it is, you've felt it since that bar in New York. I know it's fast, and I know it doesn't make sense. But isn't that the point? Love isn't supposed to make sense."

"Love?" she blurted out with a nervous laugh. "This isn't love, Mats."

"It's not? You're telling me you don't feel as drawn to me as I am to you? That you don't crave my touch like I do yours? Remi, I can barely be in the same room as you without wanting to rip off your clothes. And I think you feel the same."

"Lust isn't love, Mats."

"Lust?"

Remi turned and rushed to the kitchen, putting some distance between them so she could think straight.

"I'm not saying I'm not drawn to you. Obviously, I am. But, I'm leaving and-"

"And what? And that's it? You're going to fly away, and we'll never see each other again?"

He looked hurt. Genuinely hurt and she wanted desperately to go to him. But she knew she had to stay strong.

"It'll suck, sure. I'll miss you. But, I'll be back at some point, and we can-"

"We can meet up and fuck, and then you leave again? Gone for another six months where I'm supposed to just wait around for you?"

"No. Of course not."

"And the other men? Those fun guys you fuck all over the world. What about them?"

Her eyes met his, and she felt a sudden stab in her gut.

"I...I can't do this, Mats. I can't-"

"Right," he declared, moving to the door. She watched him slide his boots on and grab his coat. He marched out without looking at her.

TWENTY-EIGHT

An hour went by before Remi called him. She took a breath, ready to argue, but heard his phone buzzing from the couch. Unsure of what to do, she went to the balcony and peered over, hoping to see him pacing or heading back home.

She hadn't meant to hurt his feelings, but he needed to know that she wasn't here for a relationship, right?

Why? A voice in her head asked.

Remi moved back inside and found her way into the bedroom. She sat on the bed and started to pick at her nails.

Why? The voice asked again.

Because I'm not that girl. I'm the fun one who flies around and has crazy sex with gorgeous men. I'm not some cliché who needs a man to be happy. I like my life. I love New York, and I love seeing the world. I can't just stop all that because this guy shows up.

I mean, do I want him? Sure.

Do I crave his touch? …yes.

Did I feel something deep down from the second his hand touched mine and spend that whole flight picturing his cock in my mouth and wondering what it would be like to fuck him, and am I sitting here now, missing him and wondering what a life with him would be like? Huh?

Fuck! Yes, OK? Yes. But that doesn't mean...I can't just become someone else all of a sudden. Can I?

Her eyes fell on the box in his closet, and she bit her lip as an idea formed. Quickly, she made the bed, smoothing the covers and propping the pillows in place.

Then, she grabbed the box and found the lingerie she'd seen. It was tiny and more like a bodysuit, full of leather straps, and had a pair of crotchless panties attached. Luckily, the tag was still on, so she knew nobody else had used it.

One by one, Remi pulled out the toys she felt she would be comfortable with, including the double penetration strap-on and a bottle of warming lube. Then, she yanked the blinds and found some candles in the living room, setting them up away from the bed.

After lighting the candles, she stripped out of her clothes and pulled the tag off the lingerie. It was snug, but that just meant her tits looked amazing. There were a couple of snaps in the back that she struggled with, but soon enough, she was dressed...or undressed, as it were.

The thing covered her nipples, just barely, with silk falling over her hips. The crotchless panties looked amazing, framing her ass while giving total access. Finally, she grabbed the heels she had in her case and tousled her hair a little.

Once she was ready, she made her way over to the bed, grabbing one of the straps and attaching it to his headboard. She added the second one to the other side, suddenly disappointed that he didn't have anywhere to strap her legs.

Not knowing when he'd be back, Remi perched on the bed, her arms free but ready to put one in the strap at a moment's notice. Luckily, she'd brought her phone because it was another hour before he walked through the door.

Remi kept quiet, buckling her left hand into the strap and tossing her phone on the nightstand. She stretched her legs out and crossed her ankles before changing her mind and bringing them up, turning until she was on her knees.

"Remi?" She heard him call.

When she was in place, she invited him in. He walked through the bedroom door with his head down, an apology on his lips. But that fell away when he looked up to see her kneeling on the bed, legs apart and one hand strapped to the bedpost.

"What are you doing?" he urged, staying put in the doorway.

"I thought we could play," she breathed, taking her other hand and running it over her nipple. "I wanted to try some of your toys," she added, nodding to the table.

His eyes widened, and she could see he wanted to come to her. But he shook his head and turned. Quickly, Remi undid her wrist and rushed to catch him.

"Hey, Mats. Come on," she whispered, reaching up to his face.

"Remi, I-"

She put a finger to his lips and shushed him, using her other hand to guide him to her groin. His fingers were cold against her as she moved them into her pussy. He licked his lips and eyed the outfit, his eyes needy and dark.

"Come on. I want to play," she said again, gasping a little when his fingers grazed her clit.

Before he could argue, she pulled at him, walking back until they were in the bedroom. Then, she left him, moving until her legs hit the bed, at which point she turned and bent over.

His breath caught when he saw her pussy framed in the panties.

She made it to the head of the bed and lifted her finger, beckoning him to her. She let her legs fall open and dropped her other hand to her pussy. He glanced at the toys before locking his eyes on her wetness, watching her stroke herself for a few seconds before finally giving in.

"Lift your hands up," he huffed, moving forward and towering over her.

He ran a hand over her breasts, then trailed it to between her legs, where he found her hot and damp.

"You feel ready, Remi," he said, taking his hand away so he could restrain her.

"I am."

"Why is that?" Mats walked around the bed and fixed her other hand in place.

"I want you," Remi answered honestly.

He moved to the end of the bed and tugged on her

ankles, pulling until her arms were up over her head. When he pushed her right leg aside, she took in a breath, preparing herself for his tongue.

But it never came. He positioned himself between her legs but didn't touch her. Instead, he slowly removed his sweater and shirt. Only then did he put his hands on her thighs, gripping them as he lowered his face to her groin.

The second his tongue made contact, she pulled against the restraints, moaning, and wriggling as he licked and sucked without mercy. He went in hard and fast, pushing her to the edge within just a couple of minutes.

Her breathing became short, and he heard the familiar moan of an almost-orgasm, before promptly moving away, leaving her needy and annoyed.

"Not so fast." Mats climbed back and stood, striding around to where she'd laid out the toys. His eyebrow raised when he saw the strap on.

"This is what you want, Remi?"

"Yes, Mats."

"How much do you want it?" he asked, slowly pulling his pants down.

Her eyes were on his dick as she responded. "I need it."

He nodded and bent down, kissing her softly as he pinched at her nipple. "Let's have some fun, then."

TWENTY-NINE

Mats took his time. He wasn't fully hard, but it was still a bit of a struggle to get the ring around his balls. Once it was in place, though, Remi's pussy started to hum. The thought of that second black cock ramming inside of her at the same time as Mats was too much.

Instinctively, she leaned closer, opening her mouth a little as if to invite him in. But he wagged his finger and reached for the toys. She heard a buzzing sound and clenched, straining to see what he'd picked up.

Soon enough, she felt it against her wrist, soft and humming lightly against her skin. He ran it slowly down her arm, drawing goosebumps on her flesh until he reached her breast. Quickly, he circled around and moved to other arm.

Still standing at her side, Mats turned off the vibe and lifted the blindfold off the table, gently nestling it around Remi's head. She felt him come closer, his breath warm just before he kissed her, keeping things slow and sweet. His hand cupped her breast as his tongue slipped between her lips, and she groaned against him.

When he flicked the vibrator back on, she felt a jolt in her clit. It was right next to her nipple, which Mats promptly took in his mouth. Licking over and over, she felt his other hand on the bed near her shoulder. His knee pressed on the mattress as he leaned over to reach her other breast.

Remi twisted her hips, wanting him to touch her pussy too, but he didn't take the hint. Or rather, he ignored it.

Standing back up, Mats lifted the strap back over her right nipple and positioned the still buzzing vibe just below. It wasn't too intense, but Remi could feel her insides starting to ache.

She felt him lean over and then come back before sucking her other nipple into his mouth. When he let go, she felt cold metal on her breast as he put the clamp in place. Already knowing what she liked, he tightened it until she panted and moaned. Then he moved to the other, taking the vibe away and biting at her before putting the other clamp on.

When they were both deliciously pinching at her, he let out a breath, and she felt him stand up. She tried to follow the sound of his feet, but he'd left the vibe buzzing on the bed, so it was all she could hear.

A few seconds later, she felt something cold against her warmth. Remi puffed and tried to sit up, but he held her leg down and pressed it harder. Mats ran the thing through her lips and across her pussy, the cold making her nipples even harder, which made the clamps pinch even tighter.

"Oh, god," she whimpered when he slipped it inside.

But he only gave her a few strokes before pulling it

away again. Then she felt the lube, cold at first, but as his fingers massaged her, it started to warm. Finally, Remi felt the thing at her opening again as well as something close to the clit.

The other vibe suddenly stopped, and she felt his knee on the bed between her legs. In one quick movement, Mats slipped the horseshoe-shaped toy inside, rubbing over her clit as it moved. He expertly guided it in and out, keeping it on her mound the whole time.

A new hum found her ears, and she called out as the vibe started to press against her clit. Mats kept the movement steady, pressing into her, and she heard him breathing harder.

His hand and the toy slid over her most sensitive spot, slipping in and out as it buzzed against her G-spot. It wasn't long before she started to feel an orgasm building.

Remi tried to keep her breathing under control, knowing that if he knew she was close, he'd pulled away, leaving her on the edge and begging for more. But it was no use. Mats picked up the pace, his breathing increasing with each stroke.

As she rose, she started to gasp and moan, right until he pulled the toy free, leaving her cold and absolutely devastated.

"Fuck. *Mats*! Fuck."

He heaved off the bed, and she felt his hand on the blindfold. When he raised it up, she saw his fingers wrapped around his cock. It was glistening in the candlelight from the lube, and she suddenly knew why he'd been breathing so hard.

Mats stood over her stroking his dick, watching her greedy eyes take him in. Then he reached down and gave a few hard tugs on her nipples, which made her legs pull up.

When she looked back at him, he was holding a new toy.

In the heat of the moment, she'd pulled out a cute-looking crop. It was black leather with a heart-shaped, fluffy top, and before all this started, it seemed like a good idea. But now, all she wanted was his thick dick inside of her.

With his free hand, Mats untied her closest hand. Then he stalked around the bed and undid her other, letting her arm fall. Sweetly, he kissed them both, running his hand over the red marks.

"Does it hurt?" he asked, his eyes dark.

"No, it's fine."

"Good. Now get on your knees."

Remi did as she was told, turning so she was facing him. He stood and moved his hips, positioning himself right in front of her face.

Not needing to be told twice, Remi took his whole length in her mouth. She wasn't slow or sweet. Instead, she sucked him all the way in and ran her tongue roughly over the tip. Mats shuddered and groaned, his hand suddenly in her hair.

The strap on he was wearing attached around his penis and balls. The black dildo hung underneath, parallel to Mats 'dick, while a small bullet vibe sat on top. It made it difficult to use her hands, but Remi wasn't a quitter.

Soon enough, he started to swell in her mouth, his moaning getting louder the more she sucked and swirled. She felt him lean, the crop brushing gently over her ass before he brought it down hard on her right butt cheek.

Remi pushed out a small breath, keeping his cock in her mouth as he spanked her again. Then, he leaned further, and she felt his hand in her pussy as she worked on his ever-expanding dick. The crop hit her again, somehow just shy of her clit. It stung, and she felt the pain all the way up to her nipples, which were still pinched and throbbing.

Suddenly pulling away, Mats put his hand under her chin and lifted her into a kiss. She felt the two cocks against her thigh and pulled him back until they fell onto the bed.

Mats raised himself up and brushed the hair from her face, locking his eyes on her before licking at her lips and tugging on her nipples. She closed her eyes at the sharp sensation, moaning aloud, so he knew it was good.

Eventually, Mats stretched past her and picked up the lube again. She watched as he squirted some on the dildo and then applied it to her slit. Her pussy didn't need it - she knew she was soaked. But she was grateful for the extra help at the back.

He lifted her hips and moved her legs as wide as she'd allow, his fingers finding her clit and pinching at it as his other hand pulled on her clamps. Then she felt him at her openings.

He got the dildo in place and pushed gently, getting the tip inside just as his dick reached her pussy. She felt it enter, the dildo moving further as he pressed in.

Unlike the plug, this feeling was on a whole other level. The two cocks moved in tandem, filling her agonizingly slowly, the nerves in both passages coming to life all at once.

After he'd gone as deep as he could, Mats pulled back, a little faster this time before thrusting in again. He kept his hands on her thighs, pushing her wide open.

"Talk to me," Mats breathed.

"Don't stop," Remi moaned. "Fuck me, don't stop."

She put her hand on his wrist and squeezed, pulling him in the hopes he'd get the message.

He did. Mats picked up the pace, thrusting harder and faster with each stroke. Every time he filled her, she felt overwhelmed. It was like nothing she'd ever felt before, and she never wanted it to end.

The harder he pushed, the closer Remi got. Her G-spot was being thoroughly spanked thanks to the tighter hold she had on Mats, and she knew that if he touched her clit, it wouldn't take long before she came.

As his speed picked up, Mats let go of her thighs, falling onto his hands and leaning over her. He licked at her straining nipples and used one hand to tug. She groaned his name, and he pulled again, moving back and forth until she cried out.

Then he pulled one free with his teeth, causing a jolt of pain to reach her clit. He kept up his pounding as he moved to her other breast, licking and tugging.

When his hand then found her clit, Remi thought she might pass out. It was all too much. The feeling of being doubly penetrated with the clamps and now her clit…it was all she could do to keep breathing right.

Mats was driving into her, his fingers roughly dragging over her nub as he tried to prop himself up on the one hand. She could hear his breathing was short and knew he was just as close.

She felt it too and reached to her breast, tugging on the remaining clamp until the very last second. Right as she reached her peak, she pulled it, screaming out as she came. Mats fucked her harder, his hand still on her clit until he finally groaned and twitched and fell on top of her.

Remi couldn't move even if she wanted to. So, she wrapped her arms and legs around him and waited until they could both breathe again.

THIRTY

Things more or less went back to normal after they showered. Mats was his usual, sweet self, and Remi felt like she could relax again. They made lunch together and watched more home renovation shows while they ate.

Remi kept her phone on silent, not wanting a call from the airline to ruin the mood. Though, she assumed that the flights were still canceled since it was past noon already.

She and Mats kept things light, talking about their families and friends, not going deeper to avoid another argument. Though, she wanted to ask what he was really thinking. What had he decided on his little walk?

When her phone lit up on the couch, Remi snatched it up and said she had to pee. She shut the door and kept her voice low.

"Scott."

"Captain Scott, I'm sorry you didn't get a call sooner, but we were waiting on Arlanda to give us a final answer."

"Ok…and?"

"And-" the young woman sighed "-the

temperature plummeted, and now they've got ice. Of course, they can work around that, but it'll take some time to prep the aircraft, and they won't be resuming any flights until the morning. As of right now, you should be heading out around noon, but that might change. Keep your-"

"Phone charged and close by. Yeah. OK."

Tomorrow. Remi took a deep breath and held it in, wondering how best to broach the subject with Mats.

"Hey, what are you thinking for the rest of the day?" he asked as she came out, her phone behind her back and a smile on her face. "I'm happy to stay put, but if you want, we could take a walk into the city. It's not that far, and they're good about salting the streets. We could grab dinner near the Old Town?"

Remi smiled and nodded. "Yeah. That sounds nice."

Luckily, she had black pants and a nice sweater, which she promptly covered up with a plush scarf and one of Mats 'thick coats. She donned her boots again, and the pair made their way out into the chill.

She could see where the sun had melted the snow and then where the cold had frozen it. But now, there were more people out, walking with purpose, like it was any other day.

"Is everything just open again?" she asked as they passed an ice cream shop.

"Yeah. We're used to this weather, so it's not really an excuse to stay home for more than a day or two."

Remi chuckled and then looked up to him. "Should *you* be at work?"

He smiled and pulled her close. "I can work from home. It's fine."

"Mats-"

"Remi, don't worry. I just got back from a trip, remember? As far as they know, that was six days of non-stop work. They can do without me for a day or two."

They took a slight right, away from the water and towards a small park. It was full of kids and snowmen. Then, a little further, they reached a bigger road, and Remi was amazed to see it all but clear and traffic moving along like normal.

They followed along, walking quietly, hand in hand until she saw a bridge up ahead. She pulled her coat around her neck, the wind whipping at them as they made their way over the water.

In the middle, Mats squeezed her hand, stopping her as he pulled out his phone.

"Let's take a picture," he said, pulling her under his arm and lifting his phone to take a selfie.

Remi smiled at the pretty setting, with the snowy river and stone buildings in the background. When Mats kissed her, she leaned into him, her gloved hand on his chest. She heard the camera click again and was kind of shocked when she saw the snap.

They looked like a couple. A real couple who'd been together for years. Happy and in love.

Shit.

Across the bridge, they followed the main road into the city before taking a right. Stockholm city center was a stunning blend of new and old. The modern, glass skyscrapers sat beside beautiful old stone buildings. Trams rolled through the streets, and they passed everything from fine dining restaurants to McDonald's and Starbucks.

When they reached the water again, Remi stopped and let out a low, "Whoah."

"Stockholm is known for all these little islands. That's the Parliament House."

Across from where they stood, over a small bridge, sat a beautiful stone building with a curved exterior and wall full of windows. It seemed to float on an island of its own. Further from that, across another bridge and more water sat more stone buildings that were like nothing she'd ever seen in the states.

"It's so beautiful," Remi breathed as they strolled.

"That's the Old Town," Mats said, gesturing towards the end of the bridge. "Cobbled streets and little shops."

They spent the next hour meandering through the streets. It looked a little bit like Valencia or Paris, with the narrow walkways and colorful buildings. Of course, each city had its own personality and charm, but many European cities looked like cousins, drawn from a similar plan.

She told Mats that she was feeling hungry, and he tugged her down a side street. It narrowed to an unbelievably small space, and they had to walk in single file to get through. At the other end, they walked out onto a small square. Mats retook her hand and led her to a restaurant on the corner.

"This place has some great local stuff," he

whispered in her ear as the host walked them to a table.

Remi opened the menu and immediately looked up to grab the waiter's attention.

"Hi, sorry, but do you have an English copy?"

He shook his head, continuing on to the kitchen.

"Huh," she said, pursing her lips. "I know I haven't seen much here, but it doesn't look like you guys cater to foreigners."

He shrugged and nodded. "Yeah, it's rare to see anything but Swedish on menus, to be honest. I'd never really thought about it before."

"Ok, so, looks like it's on you. Don't fuck this up," she joked, closing her menu and clasping her hands together.

Mats laughed and turned his attention to the food, running his finger down the choices and making sounds of surprise and approval. When the waiter came back, he ordered in Swedish without asking Remi a thing. The young man took the menus and left, leaving Remi with nothing to do but smile.

"Confident?"

He moved his head a little, lifting his hand and giving her a "so-so" gesture. "I think I know you well enough."

She couldn't help but smile when beer arrived in front of her. "So far, so good."

"Where do you like to go at home? Favorite food or place?" Mats asked, sipping his pint.

Rem blew out a breath and chewed her lip while she thought. "Suse and I have a couple diners we like.

They're close, cheap, and the food is good. I guess, if I'm, like, *going out*," she emphasized the words and raised her eyebrows to suggest something more than a casual dinner, "I'll head to a hole in the wall in Little Italy. Pretty much anything down there is worth the trip."

Mats nodded and added, "So...not Olive Garden?"

Remi laughed and admitted, "Hey man, nothing wrong with the Olive Garden. In a pinch, you can't beat those breadsticks. But those places are such tourist traps, ya know. Like, I'd *love* to go to the Cheesecake Factory more, but it's loaded with fucking foreigners." She smirked and took a sip of her beer when his eyes shot up. "They're the worst."

"Yeah," he agreed. "Foreigners coming to your country and complaining that the menu isn't is their language. What assholes."

"OK, OK. I was kidding. But those places are always full. I guess I like to try new stuff, which is almost always popping up in Brooklyn. It's a long trip, but so is getting anywhere in Manhattan these days."

"Hmm, I noticed."

Before their entrees arrived, Mats excused himself and went to the bathroom, and Remi took the opportunity to check her phone. Her heart dropped when she opened the email with her flight information for the following day:

- ARN -> JFK 11:50 -

All at once, she felt a knot form in her stomach. As

she put the phone back in her bag, she couldn't help but feel a pang of sadness, and it was all she could do to hold back the tears.

"Remi?" Mats put his hand on her shoulder as he came back to the table, staying on his feet until she looked up at him.

"Oh, I'm fine. I just got something in my eye when the door blew open." She made a show of getting a mirror and checking her eye for debris. Mats seemed to buy it and took his seat, his face lighting up when their food arrived.

"Wow," Remi cried when the plate full of meat and bright veggies was placed in front of her. "This looks amazing."

For a second, she thought about telling him and letting him know early, so he wouldn't be as surprised later. But seeing the dumb-happy look on his face as he took his first bite, she just couldn't do it.

THIRTY-ONE

By the time they finished dinner, drinks, and dessert, Remi was stuffed. She was glad for the walk home, knowing that, in her current state, she'd be in no mood to go to bed.

At some point on the way, Mats got a call. He had a quick conversation in Swedish, laughing and keeping his arm around her shoulder. When he hung up, he apologized.

"Sorry. Just work."

"Everything OK?" Remi asked, her mind on her impending flight home.

"Um, I think I might have to go into the office tomorrow," he began, looking her way. "Have you heard anything about Arlanda?"

There it is. Time to fess up, bitch.

"Uh, yeah, actually. I got an email." She kept her eyes down as she spoke, her arm still around his waist. "My flight is scheduled for around noon tomorrow."

Immediately, he pulled away.

"You have a flight? Why didn't you tell me?"

Remi looked around and closed the gap between them, tugging on his coat as she spoke.

"I just didn't want to ruin dinner. I was gonna tell

you when we got home."

Mats glanced up the street, anger on his face. When he looked back at her, he nodded and took her hand, continuing towards his apartment in silence.

In the elevator, Remi stole a glimpse his way, but he kept his eyes forward, and his chin raised. He was pissed, and he wasn't hiding it. Stepping inside, she had half a mind to grab her bag and leave. It would be so much easier.

"Mats," she said softly as he walked toward the kitchen. "Are you just not talking to me now?"

He didn't respond, instead grabbing two glasses and pulling some wine out of the fridge.

"Mats? Maybe I should just go?"

Remi watched as he poured some wine and drank it all before pouring again. She nodded and hurried to the bedroom, snatching up her clothes and stuffing them in the suitcase. He stayed in the kitchen, not saying a word as she slipped into the bathroom to grab her toothbrush.

He let her get all the way to the door before he spoke, his voice low and oddly calm.

"What if I told you that I...that I think I'm falling in love with you?"

The words were like a punch in the gut. Remi almost stumbled back, a breath shooting from her lungs.

"What?"

"I've never felt like this before, Remi. I've never felt so connected to someone so fast and-"

"Mats, it's been - what? Three days? Stop it. OK?

Just stop. You're not in love with me. You're in *lust.* You love my tits and my pussy, and you love fucking me but-"

He moved fast, almost charging her until he had her in his arms.

"Don't do that. This isn't just about the sex. You know it's not."

He searched her face, no doubt hoping for an admission that she felt the same. Like a coward, she dropped her eyes and spoke to his chest.

"I already told you that I can't do this. I can't be what you want me to be. I live in New York, remember?"

He let out a frustrated breath and put his hand on her chin, lifting her face until he could see her eyes.

"What do you think I want you to be that you aren't already? I want *you,* Remi. I want all of you exactly as you are. That's who I've fallen in l-"

She put her hand over his mouth before he could say it. If he did, she wasn't sure she'd have the strength to walk out the door.

"I'm sorry, Mats." Remi reached up and kissed him. "I just can't."

He pushed back, running a hand through his hair and raising his voice.

"That's bullshit, and you know it. Why are you trying so hard to fight this?"

Remi could feel her heart racing. She felt the knot in her stomach, and her eyes started to water.

"Remi? What are you so afraid of?"

"I don't want to just be someone's wife. I don't

want to just be someone's mom. OK? Do you know how many women I've known who fell in love and got married and just lost themselves? They became unrecognizable just to fit into that perfect little box, and I *won't* let that be me."

Mats opened his mouth and shook his head in confusion. "Why do you think I want you to change?"

She waved her hand and rolled her eyes. "You *think* you don't want me to change. But what happens when you have some important work thing I have to fly to Bangkok? What happens when your sister gets married, and I'm on a flight to London?"

"Wait, slow down. Who's talking about marriage? When did I ever say that?"

"You know what I mean. You'll be fine with it for a while. But little by little, you'll start to expect me to be home more and to be available more, and then you'll want kids and-"

His laughter broke her concentration, and she stood, mouth open, fists balled, watching him mock her.

"Remi," he said, taking a couple of steps closer. "Just because I'm telling you that I...care about you doesn't mean I'm expecting you to move here. I'm not demanding some declaration and grand gesture. All I want is for you to admit that you maybe, *possibly* care about me too. And that *maybe* we can try to make this work."

His casual tone and logical thinking threw her. All of a sudden, she felt ridiculous.

Remi backed away and put her hands in her hair.

He was making sense, but she *knew* how this would end. She'd fall, and he'd be amazing - at first. But then the distance would be too much, and he'd expect her to come to Stockholm all the time.

It can't work.

"I'm sorry, Mats. I think I should just go now." She turned and grabbed her coat, slipping her feet into her boots and reaching for the door without zipping them up.

"Remi? Are you serious? You're just gonna walk away from me? From what this might be?"

A big part of her wanted to stay. To toss her things on the ground and rush into his arms. She wanted him to tear her clothes off and fuck her against the wall. She wanted to feel his cock inside as he sucked at her nipple. To feel that release in the way that only he could give her.

But before she knew it, she had her coat on, and her boats zipped up. She picked up her bag and met his eyes one last time before smiling and reaching her hand out. He stayed put, his face a mix of angry and upset.

"Maybe I'll be back soon," she offered weakly.

Mats opened his mouth, but nothing came out. His jaw clenched, and she thought she saw a glisten in his eyes. Remi walked out before her own tears started to fall.

THIRTY-TWO

One week later

"Good mornings, ladies and gentlemen, and welcome to London Heathrow. You'll be happy to hear that we've arrived 12 minutes ahead of schedule and the weather today looks beautiful. As I mentioned earlier, we will need you all to keep your seats as we let the security agents on board. Hopefully, this won't take too long. From all of us here at Atlântica Airways, thank you so much for your understanding. We hope you have a pleasant onward journey, and we hope to see you all again soon."

Remi rolled her eyes as the head attendant made his announcement.

"Except you 13B. You can go fuck yourself," she huffed.

Chris laughed and shook his head beside her. "I still don't get how he got *that* drunk so fast. What a twat."

"Who the hell knows. He could've been wasted before he even got here. Functioning alcoholics are good at hiding it, right?"

Remi left the rest to Chris and made her way

into the cabin. She nodded through the window and the security guards and glanced back to where the problem passenger sat.

For all his bravado, he suddenly looked pretty sheepish. When they were given the all-clear, one of her flight crew unlocked the door and stepped back to allow four beefy guys on board. They quickly made their way to row 13.

She'd been hoping for a scuffle. The guy was rude and arrogant and had been pretty damn abusive to her staff. She'd been close to clocking him once or twice but managed to keep her cool when he woefully agreed to retake his seat.

Still, it would've made all their days to see him dragged away kicking and screaming.

"Not so tough anymore, huh?" Sam whispered as the guy calmly stood and followed the men off the aircraft.

He kept his head low as they escorted him up to the gate and toward the security area. Remi rolled her eyes and sighed, already sick of London.

"These flights would be a lot more pleasant without the passengers, huh?"

Sam chuckled and reached for the intercom, announcing to the rest of the plane that they could stand and disembark. Most people smiled and expressed their gratitude, but a few made their distaste known. Of course, being mostly British, nobody actually said anything. Just a stiff upper lip and a slightly sour expression.

Once she and her crew were through immigration,

Remi relaxed her shoulders and pulled out her phone. She hadn't switched it on since they left, so she stood waiting for the minibus with her cheek in her teeth and her foot tapping.

She'd texted Mats a couple of times over the last week, and he hadn't replied. She'd figured he would still be mad, but it had to pass at some point, right?

"Still nothing from Lover Boy?" Chris nudged her arm and glanced at her phone as it sprang to life.

Remi regretted telling him anything about her time in Stockholm, but she especially wished she'd kept how she'd left to herself. Chris seemed far too invested in her love life, and it was starting to drive her crazy.

"I wasn't even checking for that," she mumbled as she handed her bag to the driver.

"Why don't you just call him?"

Because I have! I have called, and he won't fucking answer!

"Why would I call him? It was a one-night stand that turned into a three-night stand. It's not a big deal."

She hopped up the steps before he could say anything and put her bag and coat on the seat beside her. Chris took the hint and found a chair a few rows back. He started chatting to another pilot from Australia, leaving Remi to begrudgingly re-read the texts she'd sent over the last few days.

HEY. HOW'S IT GOING?

LOOK, I JUST WANTED TO SAY I'M

THREE NIGHTS IN STOCKHOLM

SORRY. I SHOULDN'T

HAVE LEFT LIKE THAT. CAN WE TALK?

--

HEY AGAIN. SO, I GUESS YOU'RE

STILL PISSED. I GET IT. I WAS AN ASSHOLE.

I WAS JUST SITTING HERE THINKING ABOUT

HOW YOU BENT ME OVER YOUR KITCHEN COUNTER.

WHAT ABOUT YOU?

--

SO I JUST GOT BACK FROM MIAMI.

ALWAYS FUN TO WORK A WEEK OF ROUND-TRIPS

FOR DRUNK COLLEGE KIDS AND CRUISE MOMS.

LUCKILY I'LL BE ON A ROUTE TO
LONDON ON MONDAY.

HOW HAVE YOU BEEN?

She felt a wave of humiliation as she read her words and felt the desperation. *What the fuck, Remi?* She'd never chased a guy before, so why start now?

"Get it together," she whispered under her breath.

It was time to let Stockholm go. Time to get back to being the old Remi. The fun Remi. The Remi who went out to a bar or club, found a hot guy, and took him home without knowing his name.

Luckily, London was the perfect place to get over her slump.

She took a quick shower at the hotel and slipped

into her skinniest jeans, high heels, and a top that was cut very low. She ordered a cab and made her way into the city, hair flawless and lipstick perfect.

It had been a while since her last trip to the UK, and when she got to her favorite bar, she found her usual fuck buddy was gone. The girl behind the bar apologized and handed Remi her drink with a shrug. But she wasn't going to let that stop her.

After a couple of drinks, a group of guys came in. They looked like they were there on a lunch break. Their suits all but matched, and they all had the same fuckboy haircut and designer stubble.

Still, one grabbed her eye. He was a couple of inches taller than her, with light blonde hair and a tattoo peeking out from under his collar. He caught her staring and smiled, looking to his side to see if she was checking out his friend. Remi looked down at her drink and then back up. She smirked a little and tilted her head, and he took the bait.

She watched him excuse himself, and when he stood, she got a better look at his profile. He wasn't the tallest, but he looked big and strong. Rugby, maybe?

"Alright?" he said with a smile as he arrived at her side.

"Yeah, I'm good. How about you?"

He raised his eyebrow and glanced back. "American, ey?"

"Guilty."

"Mind if I sit?"

Remi waved her hand and turned, so she was facing him.

"So, you here on holiday, or..."

"Work, actually."

"Oh yeah? What do you do then?" he asked, lifting his hand to order them both another round.

"I'm a pilot. I work for Atlântica Airways."

"Bloody hell, a pilot? Don't think I've ever met a pilot."

Remi shrugged and smiled at the bartender as she slid over a fresh drink. "What about you?"

"Oh, I work in insurance. Boring, really."

"Well, here's to boring." She laughed and raised her glass. "Sometimes boring is good, trust me."

His interest peaked, Remi told him all about the drunk guy on the flight. He then went on to ask about her other flights and places she'd been. He seemed genuinely interested, though his eyes fell to her chest every chance they got.

After an hour or so, his friends got up and left. Bro code intact; they didn't interrupt.

Remi took it as an opportunity. "So, you live close by?"

His eyes widened for a second before he nodded enthusiastically. "Yeah. Like a ten-minute walk."

"I could use a walk," Remi whispered, handing her card to the bartender.

When the bill was paid, she grabbed her jacket and stumbled out into the sunshine. It was the middle of the day, and she was six drinks in. The guy wasn't much better himself, having moved onto whiskey when he saw she was drinking bourbon.

It took a little longer than ten minutes, but they

finally arrived at a row of terraced houses. He let her in, and they tripped and faltered their way upstairs to another door. The place had been split into two apartments, and it was just as she'd imagined.

Leather couch, no cushions, giant TV, dishes in the sink, clothes on a chair. She excused herself to the bathroom and found a wet towel on the floor and beard hair in the sink.

This guy wasn't her type. Yes, she went home with guys all the time, having only just met them. But talking with him in the bar had been a struggle. He seemed to have very little to say.

Determined to power through, Remi fixed her tits and tried to shake off the booze. When she toppled back out, he was already shirtless. She could see he was trying to flex and stifled a laugh.

Just get through it, and you'll be back to your old self.

He moved in and grabbed her, pulling her in for a kiss that was way too rough to be considered sexy. His sloppy tongue flopped into her mouth, and his hand squeezed her tit like it was a stress ball.

Just think about Séb. Think about Risto. Think about...no. Think about Risto and his cock. His big, perfect cock.

They fell back onto the couch, and he went straight for her pants, tugging the skinny jeans down and pushing her panties aside. He jammed his fingers between her dry folds, moving them back and forth without any thought or lubrication.

Remi put her hand on his and rolled them over, trying to slow things down so she could get in the mood. But this guy was all hands and dick. He basically bucked her off as he shuffled out of his pants, his dick popping free and falling over to one side.

With a sigh, Remi stood and put her hands on her breasts. She tweaked at her nipples and sauntered back, hoping he'd take the hint and follow. Eventually, he did. He stood and stroked his cock as he followed her to his bedroom, which was covered in yet more clothes and a couple of empty pizza boxes.

Remi crawled on the bed and rolled onto her back. She sucked on her fingers before gently touching herself, hoping it would be enough to help him out.

He leaped onto the bed and kissed her again, his dick poking at her as he tried to find her opening.

Remi rolled her eyes and reached down, guiding him in. He groaned and thrust into her, the little lubrication she'd applied not doing much to ease her discomfort.

Think about Paris and being tied to that curtain rod. Séb's cock and how he always teases you before ramming in like he's desperate for only you. Fucking Risto in the park. The feeling of his fingers on your clit. In the car. Anyone could've seen.

Since this guy didn't seem to care, Remi licked her fingers again and moved her hand between them. She carefully applied her saliva around his dick, making things a little more pleasant. Then she started to rub on her clit, images of Séb and Risto going through her mind.

But it wasn't enough. She was barely even wet, and he was already close.

Mats. Fuck, Mats.

Closing her eyes, Remi pictured his face. The way he looked at her at the airport bar. His piercing eyes and that smirk as he talked about pleasing her. She bit her lip as she remembered the way he felt. The toys and the cold and his hands all over her.

All at once, Remi felt her orgasm building. She worked her clit harder, squeezing her eyes shut as she tried to picture Mats above her.

Mats' dick deep inside.

Mats' fingers roughly dragging over her mound

She just wanted to cum before this asshole got off, but his sad little cock just wasn't doing it for her.

He started to move even faster, his body pressing against her as she roughly worked herself. He came in a shout and a shudder, but Remi kept rubbing, ignoring him completely until she finally came.

The guy rolled off and laughed, no doubt high-fiving himself in his head. Remi came down from her high fast, annoyed, unsatisfied, and worst of all, missing Mats.

As quickly as she could, she rinsed off and got dressed, ordering a cab before she was even out the door. On her way back to her hotel, she closed her eyes and let the anger and sadness wash over. The driver kept his eyes on the road as she tried to hold back the tears.

What the fuck am I supposed to do now?

THIRTY-THREE

When the taxi turned towards the hotel, Remi hesitated. She saw Chris out front with a couple of the flight attendants and decided she wasn't in the mood for a chat.

"Could you pull around back?"

He did as he was asked, dropping her by the back door and accepting her tip without so much as a nod. Remi waited for the car to leave and quickly snuck round to the side door, heading straight to the elevator with her eyes on the ground.

"Remi?"

His voice stopped her in her tracks. She swung around and almost tripped when she saw his face.

"Mats?"

He smiled and stood, spreading his arms with a shrug, clearly unsure of what to say. Remi glanced to where Chris stood outside and rushed closer, hoping to keep her private life away from prying gossiping eyes.

"What are you doing here?"

"You said you'd be in London," he replied with another slight shrug. "You told me where you usually stay, so I figured…I thought that we could talk-"

Remi reached her arms around his neck and pulled him in for a kiss. She felt his hands encircle her waist as he drew her closer, his tongue finding hers. She smiled against his lips and pulled away long enough to invite him upstairs.

They fell into her room, tugging at each other's clothes, laughing and struggling with buttons. Mats kissed along her jawline, nibbling at her earlobe before trailing down her neck and along her collar bone.

He shoved her to the bed, climbing on top with a growl. Then his hands slipped under her shirt, and the second they found her nipples, Remi felt a familiar ache in her pussy.

The next thing she knew, her shirt was gone, and he was leaning over her on the bed, his eyes happy as he looked down at her. Mats pulled her bra down and captured her nipple in his mouth. Remi groaned and entangled her hand in his hair. With his free hand, Mats worked under her jeans and panties. She felt his fingers in her sex and heard him chuckle.

"You're always ready for me," he mumbled, coming back up to her lips.

Remi moaned as he found her clit, stroking and rubbing as best as he could within the constraint of her skinny jeans. When he slid his fingers inside, she cried out his name - but then stopped herself short, frozen under his touch.

The realization of where she'd just been hit her hard, and she knew why she felt so wet. It wasn't Mats; it was the guy from before. Foolishly, they hadn't used a condom, and she suddenly felt sick at the thought of

Mats touching another man's cum.

"Let's shower," she whispered into his ear, wriggling out from under him before he had a chance to question her.

She took his hand and pulled him into the bathroom, tearing his shirt off and turning on the water before either of them were fully naked. Mats followed without question and struggled with her now wet jeans. When she felt his lips on her thigh, Remi clenched and reached down, pulling him up to kiss her before he could reach the apex.

His pants came down easier, and Remi sighed when she saw his thick cock standing to attention. Immediately she lifted her leg to his waist and wrapped her arms around his neck.

Mats lifted her, and she slid down onto him with ease.

"Oh, *fuck*," he groaned. "Fuck, Remi."

He started to move, thrusting up hard and fast until she began to cry out. She moaned his name and gasped when his teeth found her nipple. Too soon, she felt the pressure building inside. The feeling of him inside ramming past all those nerve endings made her clench around him tighter.

He sensed her need and lifted her other leg, stepping out of the shower and resting her ass on the edge of the sink.

With his now free hands, he found her clit and started to rub. Remi held on, his pace speeding up, his breath coming faster.

Mats ducked and leaned his head against hers.

"What do you want?" He panted, his hips never stopping the assault on her sex.

Remi's head was full and fuzzy. Her orgasm was so close she could hardly speak. Eventually, she managed to breathe. "I want you. All of you."

Mats grinned and kissed her, his hand slipping from her clit as he tried to keep balance.

"The bed," she growled. "Now!"

Mats snarled and dragged her into the bedroom. She lifted her hand to kiss him, but he was too fast, spinning her on the spot and all but tossing her onto the bed.

Remi crawled forward with her ass in the air, just until her knees were firmly in place. Mats wasted no time, his dick pushing into her before she had the chance the steady herself.

His hands gripped her hips as he pounded her from behind. Remi used the sheets for purchase, arching her back as he slipped in and out.

Too soon, she heard the telltale sign that he was close. His hand touched the bottom of her back, pressing her forward until she was face down on the bed. His dick stayed in place as he fell on top of her, his knees pushing her legs apart.

Mats slowed his pace, bringing his cock almost all the way out before ramming it back inside, drawing a tortuous moan from Remi's lips. She lifted onto her hands, arching, and twisting until she was close enough to bite his bottom lip.

Mats reached around and grabbed her breast, pinching the nipple between his fingers, and she licked and kissed him. Then he moved then down, sliding beneath her hips until he found her needy clit.

She felt his hips speed up, and he worked her in front. It was all she could do to keep her body twisted to meet his lips. But they were both greedy for each other, their tongues reaching out as they rose together.

"Harder," she breathed into his mouth.

He obliged, pounding into her as hard as he could with just one hand for support. The other found her nub and flicked and pinched until she twitched and screamed his name, her hips convulsing as he kept up his pace.

Just when she thought it would become too much, she felt another orgasm coming. A few hard thrusts later, they both came, Mats keeping his fingers where they were until she was totally spent.

After a couple of minutes, he pulled himself free and turned her around to face him. Taking her face in his hands, he sighed and smiled.

"I missed you." He sighed, leaning down for a kiss.

"I missed you, too."

Remi let Mats shower, and then she rinsed herself as thoroughly as she could. She didn't want a trace of that other guy on her while Mats was in the room.

"Hey, did you eat?" she called out while she toweled off. "Mats?"

Opening the door, she found him on the bed, a sad look on his face.

"What's wrong?"

"Were you just with another guy?"

The question threw her, and she genuinely looked confused.

How the fuck could he know that?

"What are you talking about?" she stammered.

Mats looked at the floor where her phone had fallen from her bag. She took a few steps and reached down, tapping the screen with her finger as she stood back up. Her heart sank when she read the text.

HI. IT'S JAMIE.

HOW LONG YOU IN TOWN?

MY BIG COCKS LONELY ALREADY

How the fuck did he get my number?

Closing her eyes, Remi tried to think of something to say. But when she looked at him, she knew nothing would help.

"I didn't know you were coming."

"That's it? *You didn't know I was coming?*"

The look on his face made her feel small and ashamed. He was equal parts angry and sad, but she could see he was judging her too. And that drove her fucking crazy.

"I'm sorry, but who the fuck do you think you are?"

Her sudden turnaround made him shut his mouth and furrow his brow in confusion.

"I've been texting and calling you all week, and you've ignored me. Then you just show up and expect me to be waiting? How do you figure that?"

Mats stood and started to get dressed.

"You've been texting me all week, apologizing for

how you left. I thought…I thought you wanted to try this. I thought I'd come here, and we'd talk about making this work. But instead, I find you fresh out of another man's bed and-"

"You're goddamn right. And you don't get to judge me or be mad at me for that. You're not my boyfriend, Mats. You're not…you're not anything right now. So yeah. I arrived in London, got a little drunk, and fucked some moron. And you know what, that's my fucking choice. I get to do whatever I want because I'm a grown-ass woman."

"Remi-"

"Don't *Remi* me. Maybe if you'd picked up your fucking phone in the last week, things would be different. But as it stands, you're just some guy I fucked in Stockholm. You don't get a say over my pussy."

For a second, he looked like he wanted to argue. He opened his mouth and lifted his hand, finger extended as if he wanted to make a point. But just as fast, he seemed to shrink. He picked up his stuff and walked out the door, just like she had the week before.

THIRTY-FOUR

"Remi, calm down."

"Don't tell me to calm, Suse. OK? I'm fucking pissed."

Remi looked over her shoulder and ducked her head when the waitress shot her a dirty look.

"Wanna relax a little?" Susanna scolded, her eyes narrow and her mouth a firm line.

"I'm sorry, OK? Shit." Remi downed her coffee and dropped her head in her hands. "I just…"

"You miss him," Susanna offered with a shrug. "There's no shame in that, babe."

Babe. He called me babe in the snow. It was so natural and casual. Everything with him was.

"I do miss him, and it's driving me fucking crazy. I *hate* feeling like this. I hate that I miss him and that I texted him like some desperate bitch. I hate the way we left things and that he won't answer his fucking phone. And I hate that I can't seem to get him out of my goddamn head. I mean, seriously. Is this just-"

The waitress interrupted with their food, her face just as sour as her tone.

"Club sandwich?"

Susanna raised her hand and smiled as the food

landed on the table in front of her. Remi accepted her plate without looking up, picking at the fries under the watchful eye of her best friend.

"He really just left? Like, he flew to another country to see you, and he just...left?"

Remi shook her head and sighed. "I guess. I mean, I didn't see him again, and we left the day after. I haven't called or anything, and neither has he. So I'm guessing we're basically done."

The pair stayed quiet as they ate, each lost in their own thoughts. Once Remi managed to calm, she asked, "How's *your* new man?"

She watched as a smile spread over her friend's face. It made her feel good to know she was so happy.

"He's great. Amazing, actually. Like, he's just so... intuitive. He *gets* me. And he's not all show, even though he's insanely gorgeous. He went to college and has a degree in poli-sci."

"Seriously? Do people really do that?"

"Bryan did."

Remi caught the smug grin and rolled her eyes. "What does he do again?"

"He's a photographer, and he writes for some blog or something. He sells his stuff online to magazines and stuff. It pays surprisingly well."

"Well, I'm glad he's turned out to be one of the good ones. And that you've left Troy in the trash."

"Yeah, but it does make it kinda weird if I ever go over there. I mean, I only do when we know Troy's not around, but still. I had sex in both rooms with both guys."

"That's crazy-hot, girl. I'm so proud of you."

"Speaking of proud, did I read that Atlântica is branching out to Asia?"

Remi bit her lip and nodded enthusiastically. "Oh my god, yes. And I'm one of the most senior pilots on the roster, so I get first pick! I cannot wait until they get those routes up and running. I'll fight for a trip to Thailand."

They both laughed and went back to eating. Remi let her mind move away from Mats and towards the future. *Her* future in the skies. She'd always wanted to fly long haul, and a trip to Bangkok or Tokyo would mean a solid three days to explore.

And a move into Asia meant they'd be in Australia soon enough. She'd been before but had flown commercial. Still, it was somewhere she'd been dreaming of flying to.

If I'd stayed with Mats, I couldn't just up and go to Sydney. He wouldn't want me in Thailand for half of the month. He'd want me close. He'd smother me...right?

"Hey," Suse said, pulling her back to reality. "You OK?"

Remi smiled and nodded. "Yeah. This is what I want."

THIRTY-FIVE

Two and a half months later

"Good afternoon, ladies and gentlemen, and welcome to Amsterdam. Again, I would like to apologize for the delay, and I ask that any passengers without transfer flights keep their seats until we can get onward traveling passengers on their way. The doors should be opening in the next few minutes, and you should see flight information displayed on your screen. Thank you for flying Atlântica Airways, and we hope to see you again very soon."

"Another day, another delay," Chris grumbled.

"At least the rain stopped," Remi tried.

It was dark and grey as the bus drove the crew to their hotel. The Marriott in Amsterdam was smack in the middle of the city and five-star, no less - not something most flight crews were put up in. But with the airline's partnership, it was obviously worth their while.

Remi had flown the New York to Amsterdam route before, and she'd once had a guy waiting for her in the city. He was around her height and kind of stocky, with a thick accent and sweet smile. But he'd gotten married a couple of years before, and Remi hadn't found anyone new to entertain her on her last couple of trips.

Not that she was in the mood. The truth was, she hadn't been with anyone since London. After Mats left her in the hotel, she'd sobered up and drowned her sorrows in a takeaway curry and Friends re-runs.

From there, she'd mainly stuck to short domestic routes, with one trip to Paris two weeks prior. She didn't even text Séb, who'd been hounding her for weeks. Instead, she stayed close to the hotel and wallowed.

Even now, in Amsterdam, with all the excitement of the new routes, she couldn't find the strength to go out and celebrate.

So Remi showered and changed before heading down to the hotel's restaurant early, hoping she wouldn't be spotted.

She wasn't that lucky.

"Hey, you're here?" Chris looked shocked, his eyes searching for her non-existent date.

"Where else would I be?"

He held his tongue and pulled out the seat to her left. "I mean, you usually head out. Right?"

Remi sighed and nodded to the bartender. She lifted her hand and held up two fingers before shaking her head at Chris. "I'm just tired."

"Tired. Right."

She could feel his eyes on her and wanted to scream, but she was three drinks in and feeling nicely buzzed. So, she chose to keep her cool and plastered on a smile.

"Why aren't you out? You *love* Amsterdam."

He nodded and sighed. "I do. You're right. Still super jealous, by the way," he added, nudging her elbow.

Remi smiled and let out a small breath. "I know. It's insane. I guess it pays to be the highest-ranking pilot at an airline without a family or kids."

"Come on," Chris started as their drinks arrived. "You know you didn't just get this posting because you're single. You're the best we've got, and they want *you* to spearhead the Asia route. That's a *huge* deal. They wouldn't ask you to move here if there thought for a second you weren't the right pilot for the job."

Her cheeks flushed, and she wrinkled her nose, embarrassed at his kind words. "Thanks, Chris."

"And you're moving here! That's insanely cool. Like, crazy cool. Have you found a place? I *wish* I could come along." He took a sip of his drink, and Remi looked at his face, searching his eyes. Was he serious?

"You could, you know." She took a pull on her drink and watched him react. His eyes shot her way and narrowed, suspicious but curious.

When they'd offered her the position, she'd jumped. There was no question about it, and she didn't even need time to think. The new Atlântica Airways flights to Asia and Australia would leave from Los Angeles and Amsterdam, and the airline was sending a few key senior pilots to get things moving while they worked to hire new faces.

What they hadn't told anyone yet was that there would be positions for established Atlântica First Officers too. Remi hadn't said anything to Chris because he had a big family at home, and they seemed close. Plus, he'd always gone on and on about buying an apartment in Manhattan someday.

"I could...what?" he asked, confusion covering his face.

"You could move to Amsterdam and be part of the team that leads the first flights to Asia. Just imagine the hours you could clock on all those long hauls."

"Remi...are you serious?" He reached for her arm and squeezed.

She lifted her shoulders and grabbed her phone, quickly scrolling through her e-mails until she found the right one.

Handing it over, she clarified, "I didn't think you wanted to leave the States. You even said once that your Mom hates you being away so much and that you might need to switch to shorter-"

"This is asking Captains if they have any recommendations?" Chris blurted out re-reading the email. "As in, *you* could recommend *me,* and then I could move to Amsterdam and start flights to Bangkok and Tokyo? Are you fucking kidding me? Of course I want that! Oh my god, Remi. E-mail them right now! Like, right now!"

"Whoah." She laughed, catching her phone before it fell off the table. "You need to think about it. Really think about it. It's gonna be a huge move, and you won't know anyone here."

"I'd know you!"

She smiled and nodded, finishing her drink and looking back to the bar for another.

"True, but I'm not your babysitter. It's expensive here, and you-we don't speak the language. It's gonna be hard."

"It's worth it, though, right? I mean, how could it not be?"

Remi glanced at her phone again and chuckled. "Yeah. It's more than worth it, even if it is too late," she mumbled, thinking about how ironic it was that she was moving to Europe in the next few months.

"What do you mean too late?"

Remi waved her hand and smiled. "Nothing. I didn't mean anything. I'm excited, really!"

Chris looked down and pursed his lips. He finished his drink and took a deep breath before asking, "Is this about Mr. Stockholm?"

"What?" Remi spat out, her brows furrowed and her mouth a thin line.

"Come on, Boss. You haven't been...*you* since we left Sweden. I know it's about that guy you met."

"It's...it's..." she stammered, trying to come up with some other explanation. But she was too tired and too tipsy to lie. "I guess it is, yeah."

"He really got to you, huh?"

She rolled her eyes and brushed a hand through her hair. "Somehow. Yeah. I don't know how-it's ridiculous. Three days and I-"

"Wait." Chris lifted his hand to stop her as the bartender brought another round. "You were with him the whole time we were stuck there? The *whole* three days?"

Remi nodded slowly, lifting her new drink, feeling the alcohol making her mind foggy.

"Wow. And I'm guessing it didn't end well…or?"

"You could say that."

"So…can't you just call him? I mean, you're moving so close and-"

"He doesn't wanna hear from me."

"You don't know that, Remi. Just text him."

"I did." She laughed, waving the phone in his face before tossing it on the table. "I texted, and I called because I felt bad for how I left. And he didn't reply. He didn't call me back. But you know what that fucker did? He showed up in London."

Chris sat up straight and lifted his hands in a "wait a second" gesture. "Hold up. He was in London?"

"Mmhmm. He just showed up without calling because I guess I'd told him about the flight."

"And you…fought?"

"Worse," Remi breathed. "We fucked. The only problem was I'd just come from…well, I'd been out with another guy."

Chris's eyes widened, and he bit down on his bottom lip. She could see he wanted to make a comment but wasn't sure what was appropriate.

"I was mad, OK? I was mad that he wasn't texting me back and mad at how we left things. Plus, I was mad that I gave a shit in the first place. So, I went out and met some random douchebag. Mats saw a text from the guy after, and he…ah, he left."

"Shit." Chris put his elbow on the bar and leaned in. "I mean, that sucks. But you're both grown-ups, and I'm sure if you tried-"

"I think it's just best we leave it. I'm gearing up for this move and the new routes. I'm gonna be busier than ever. And I can't wait. I really can't!"

"OK." Chris nodded and lifted his glass. "Then here's to you. Here's to Amsterdam and new routes and adventures."

Remi grinned and clinked her glass to his. She took a long drink and closed her eyes as the rum and lime warmed her throat.

"But seriously," Chris added, picking up her phone. "*Please* e-mail them back with my recommendation."

THIRTY-SIX

April

"Good morning, ladies and gentlemen, and welcome to New York."

May

"Good afternoon, ladies and gentlemen. Welcome to Tokyo. Tōkyō e yōkoso! This is our first-ever flight into Japan, and all of us at Atlântica Airways are thrilled you chose us to get you home."

"Bienvenue à Paris."

"Benvenuto a Roma."

"Good evening, ladies and gentlemen, and welcome to Bangkok. Yindī t̂xnrạb s̄ū̀ krungtheph!"

June

"Velkommen til Oslo."

"Huānyíng lái dào xiānggǎng. Welcome to Hong Kong!"

July

"Good afternoon, ladies and gentlemen, and welcome to Stockholm. The weather is sunny and a lovely 24 degrees, and the local time is 2:40 pm. On behalf of all of us at Atlântica Airways, thank you so much for choosing to fly with us."

THIRTY-SEVEN

Chris kept his eye on Remi after their arrival. As soon as they landed, he noticed a distinct change in her demeanor, and her communications with the ground team quickly became short and cold. He watched her pick up and put her phone down at least six times before they left the plane. Then, standing in line for security, she had her arms folded, and her foot was tapping.

She was not thrilled to be back in Stockholm.

But he was.

Even if she didn't take the opportunity to see the one that got away, he wasn't about to waste their two days. He all but skipped off the minibus and jammed his finger on the button in the elevator, not waiting for a couple who were a few steps behind.

The excitement was building, and it was all he could do to not jump up and down. He raced into his room and groaned as he hauled the suitcase up onto the bed. Carefully, he lifted the garment bag out and hung it up, using his hand to brush away the creases. Next, he wiped his shoes clean and grabbed the shine kit he brought along.

Stripping out of his uniform, Chris snatched up his phone and sent a quick text:

ROOM 506

As he stepped in the shower, he heard it ping in reply and felt a twitch of anticipation.

On their one and only trip to Stockholm together, Remi had met the love of her life. She'd been lucky, of course, meeting him in New York and getting to spend their whole snowy three days in his bed.

But just because Chris hadn't been able to go out didn't mean he'd just lounged around in bed all day. Instead, he'd fired up Tinder the second he caught wind of the storm, matching with a very sexy Swede named Lars after just a couple of hours.

Over the last few months, they'd exchanged photos and had transitioned to FaceTime calls. They texted every day, and even though they'd never met in person, Chris was pretty sure he was falling...hard.

So, when the opportunity presented itself to kill two birds with one stone, he jumped. Captain Franks and his wife were more than happy for the trip to London, and he was positive Remi wouldn't be able to stay away from Mats. This was her last long flight out of New York before her big move to Amsterdam and Chris 'last chance to get her back with her man. He could only hope that she'd take the bait.

That just left him and Lars.

Chris hopped out of the shower, freshly trimmed from head to toe. He fixed his hair and rushed back into the bedroom, where he grabbed the garment bag from the hook in the closet.

Before he slipped into the fresh uniform, he tapped his phone and bit his lip as he read Lars 'reply:

30 MINS

That gave him ten minutes to prepare. His suit was perfect already, but he spent a few too many minutes fixing his tie. He even shined his shoes before pinning his Atlântica Airways badge on his chest.

He just had time for one last look in the mirror before he heard a knock at the door. Filled with a mixture of excitement and fear, Chris took a couple of breaths, his hand on the door handle while he steadied himself.

What if this didn't go well?

What if they worked over text, but when it came down to the real thing, they just fizzled?

Shaking the negative thoughts away, Chris pulled the door open to reveal Lars, in all his beautiful black-haired glory. He was every bit the Viking with his bushy beard and bright blue eyes. Like most Scandinavian men, he was tall too, and when he smiled, he lit up the room.

"Hi," Chris stuttered, stepping to the side to let him in.

"Hey," Lars replied, stepping across the threshold and taking Chris' face in his hands.

He kissed him with passion, wrapping his big arms around his neck, moaning as their tongues met. Chris heard the door slam as the pair lurched back into the room. Before they reached the bed, Lars pulled back and smiled, leaning his forehead against Chris'.

"Nice to meet you."

They both laughed as Lars took a step back, admiring Chris in his uniform. He had on jeans and a simple white T-shirt under a black jacket. He looked like a male model, and all Chris wanted to do was run his tongue up the abs he knew were hiding beneath the thin material.

"You make a very sexy pilot," Lars announced eventually, stepping in and pushing his chest close.

"Thank you. You look…so fucking hot." Chris trailed off, drawing Lars in for another knee-buckling kiss.

Any fears he had about them fizzling vanished, and soon enough, Lars was tugging at Chris' jacket. It fell to the ground, and he turned his attention to the shirt, working his way down the buttons with his fingers and eyes until they both fell of Chris 'belt.

When he looked back up through his lashes, Chris felt his cock twitch. He reached forward and pushed Lars 'jacket back, reaching for the hem of his shirt before it hit the floor.

Once they were both shirtless, Chris ran his hand along the top of Lars 'jeans, stopping at the front and slipping his hand under the denim. Lars did the same, pulling Chris 'belt free before unzipping his perfectly pressed uniform pants.

They both leaned down, kicking their shoes and socks off before standing up straight, their dicks begging to be let loose.

Lars kissed Chris again, playfully biting his bottom

lip before pushing him back onto the bed. He stalked closer and crawled up his body, trailing kisses up Chris 'thighs and over his underwear. He kept going, stopping at his nipples until Chris cried out. Soon enough, their lips met again, and Lars settled in at his side, sliding his hand down Chris 'stomach.

He rubbed his giant hand over Chris 'growing cock a few times before finding his way under the waistband. He squeezed a little before he started with slow and gentle strokes up and down.

Chris groaned and reached for Lars, finding him rock hard and ready. He clumsily tugged at his underwear, freeing his cock as he moved to his knees, ready to take him in his mouth. Lars matched his movements but instead, slipped underneath until they were both face to face with what they'd been fantasizing about for months.

Lars was faster, sucking the tip of Chris' dick into his mouth greedily. His hand trailed up his thigh and around to his ass, stopping on the right cheek and squeezing.

Excited, Chris lifted Lars into his mouth and moaned at how big he felt. It wasn't long before they were each sucking and licking, hands on abs and asses, and they explored each other.

But it was all halted by a banging at the door.

"Chris?" Remi called. "Chris, are you in there?"

He coughed out a breath and dropped his head, frustrated that she couldn't have waited another hour.

"You've got to be fucking kidding me," he snarled,

looking under his shoulder to Lars, who still had hold of his throbbing cock.

"Tell me that's not your wife." Lars chuckled.

"Worse." He sighed. "It's my boss. My very angry, very sexually frustrated boss."

"Chris!"

Chris pulled himself away and grabbed one of the robes from in the bathroom. He gave Lars, who pulled the covers over his nakedness, an 'I'm sorry 'smile. Before he could open the door, Remi called again.

"Chris, I can fucking hear you. Open the damn door, so I can kick your ass."

He did, pulling it in so fast she almost fell with the force of her fists. He smiled at her and tried to keep his tone calm.

"Boss. What can I do for you?"

"Don't give me that shit," Remi started, pushing past him into the room. "I know you switched our flights, and I-oh! Oh, wow. Fuck. Hi there."

Lars laughed and waved while Chris squeezed by to get between them.

"Uh," Remi muttered, clearly distracted by the Nordic God in the bed.

"Boss?" Chris chuckled, snapping his fingers in front of her face.

"You…excuse us," she said to Lars with a smile, tugging Chris into the bathroom and slamming the door. "First of all, good for you. He's probably the most attractive man I've ever seen, and I'm really fucking happy for you."

Her tone didn't sound happy, but Chris knew her

well enough to know she meant what she said.

"But that doesn't change the fact you fucked with my schedule. I got a text from Baz thanking me for the swap. Apparently, he and his wife are having a great time in London."

Chris looked to his hands and shrugged. "What do you want me to say, Remi? You've been miserable for months, and I didn't see you-"

"I haven't been miserable! I've been...busy. For Christ's sake, I'm in the middle of moving my whole life across the Atlantic and working on the new routes *and* the old ones. What do you want from me?"

He put his hand on her shoulder and leaned closer. "You can't lie to me, Boss. I know you better than most, and I know you miss him. But you're too goddam stubborn to fix this yourself. So, yeah, I gave you a push. And if I happen to get laid too, well then, that's just a nice bonus."

She opened her mouth to speak but stopped herself, looking at the closed door, no doubt picturing the naked man in the bed.

"He's who you've been texting this whole time? The late-night calls and steamy pics?"

He couldn't help but beam, and he nodded. "We only just met for real about...oh twenty minutes ago."

Remi deflated and closed her eyes. "Shit. I'm sorry."

"Don't be sorry. Just go and talk to Mats. We both know you want to."

He could see she wanted to argue, so he brushed past her and opened the door. Lars was still in the bed, scrolling on his phone with one giant, muscular arm behind his head.

"Tell her what you told me. About Mats," Chris prompted, plopping down on the bed.

"Uh," Lars started, putting his phone on the side table before focusing his stunningly blue eyes on Remi. "Well, you love him. Or at least you think you *could* love him, yes? And it's safe to say he feels the same about you. *You lived in New York, he lives in Stockholm*," he mocked, rolling his eyes and waving off her excuses. "That's shit. You can live anywhere. *He* can live anywhere. And, now, as luck would have, you're moving. To Europe very soon, yes? If you want this, you make it work. It's simple."

Chris watched Remi as she frowned and her shoulder slumped. She'd obviously run out of fight, and it was like it all came together in her mind. Something clicked, and she smiled.

For some reason, hearing it from Lars did the trick. She nodded and bit her lip before whispering, "You're right. You're *right.* I should try. The fucker's obviously still on my mind, and I can't seem to get over him no matter how hard I try. So...maybe I need to stop trying?"

She looked from Lars to Chris as if for permission.

"Go!" They both laughed, springing her into action.

"Fuck. *OK.* I'm going!" She took a step forward and held out her hand. Chris took it and squeezed as she added, "Thanks. And have fun!"

THIRTY-EIGHT

Remi left Chris's room and raced to the elevator. She twiddled her thumbs, waiting for the doors to open, but when she stepped inside, she hesitated. Her fingers hovered over the numbers as she tried to decide what to do.

I should just go back to my room. This is stupid. He probably doesn't wanna see me. Why would he? If he wanted to see me, he would've called or at least texted. It's been months. It's over.

She pressed the button for her floor and made her way back to her room. Inside she sat on the bed and thought about what Chris and Lars had said. Were they right? Or were they too loved up to see the truth?

It was true that she was still hung up on Mats, and she had to admit that when she was offered the chance to move to Europe, he was the first thing to cross her mind. Since she'd last seen him in London, they hadn't spoken once, but she thought about him all the time.

She'd tried to be with other men, but it never felt right. No matter how sexy they were, she just couldn't seem to focus on them. Instead, she'd think about all the things Mats did to her and how his touch felt so different.

"Fuck it," she said eventually, opening her bag and changing into jeans and a T-shirt.

What do I have to lose?

Remi stormed down to the front desk and asked them to call her a cab. Then, she waited, chewing on her nails while she tried to come up with something to say.

"Miss Scott?" The front desk clerk called after around five minutes. "Your taxi is pulling up."

She smiled and waved her thanks before walking out to meet the car. He already had the address, so she sat back and closed her eyes. She could feel her heartbeat starting to rise and the nerves settling in.

I'll just tell him I'm sorry and I miss him. Then, he'll either fuck me or tell me to go fuck myself. Either way, at least I'll know.

They hit traffic in the city, but Remi recognized where they were. An image flashed across her mind of them in the car. His mouth on her nipple at the red light. Both horny as hell and desperate to ravage each other.

All these months later, she was still baffled by his effect on her. What made him so special? Why was she so…obsessed?

When the taxi finally pulled up outside his building, Remi took a deep breath and got out. She stood on the curb, looking up at the glass with her heart in her throat. After a few extra breaths, she moved forward and pressed the button for his apartment. Minutes went by, and she pushed again, suddenly left with all this nervous energy and nobody to talk to.

Fuck. What now?

She turned and looked up and down the street, suddenly acutely aware of how crazy she was being. Terrified he'd answer, she hurried to the other side of the road. At the railing, she closed her eyes as an overwhelming feeling of regret hit her.

I should've come here months ago. I should've followed him in London and tried to explain. I should've called and texted until he answered.

A few meters to her left, she noticed a bench. The same bench Mats has brushed snow off not too long ago. She wandered over and sat, looking at Mats' apartment building, sick to her stomach. Even if he did answer, there was no telling if he'd let her up at all.

That's if he even lives here anymore. Shit. He could've moved for all I know.

As much as she wanted to leave, something kept her on the bench. Ten minutes went by, then thirty. After an hour, Remi started to feel ridiculous.

God, you're pathetic. How long are you gonna sit here and wait for this guy?

In the end, it was another hour. She scrolled mindlessly on her phone and ignored the texts from Chris asking how things had gone. However, she did smile when he sent a shot of him and Lars in bed. They both looked pretty happy, and Remi felt a tug inside.

Just as she was thinking of giving up, his voice seemed to come from nowhere, followed by a laugh. Even though he spoke Swedish, she knew it was him and lifted her eyes to the building to see Mats and a woman turning the corner.

He had his arm around her shoulders as they walked up to his door, smiling and laughing like only lovers can.

The woman put her hand on his chest and pulled him down for a kiss, her hand moving up to his cheek as they both stumbled on a grate or tile.

Instantly, Remi felt as though she'd been sucker-punched.

Panicked, she stood and turned, frantically scanning for a way to escape. To her right, and across from where they stood, was a set of steps leading to the boardwalk. Her left ended in a corner, where she'd have to cross right into their line of sight. So, she hustled to the steps, her head down and a hand covering her face.

"Remi?" His voice sounded totally shocked, and for a second, she thought about ignoring him and breaking into a run.

But she couldn't help herself. She stopped and peered up to see him and the woman watching her. She tried to smile, but even she felt it was weak. Instead, she raised a hand in a small wave before turning and taking the steps.

Remi jogged to the right as quickly as she could, heading towards the bridge and hopefully out of sight. But he was faster.

"Remi, what the fuck?" he demanded, grabbing her arm and pulling her to face him.

Catching her breath, she waved her hand

dismissively. "I'm sorry. I'm...fuck. I'm sorry. Go back to your date. I shouldn't have come here."

Mats opened his mouth and looked back, his eyes confused and suspicious.

"Is everything OK?"

For some reason, those words hit her harder than *go fuck yourself*, and she had to turn so he couldn't see the tears.

"Remi?"

"Mats, please. I made a mistake and-"

He turned her again, his hand firm on her arm. When he saw the tears, he sighed and lifted his thumb to wipe them away.

"Why don't you come up and we can talk?"

Remi shook her head, his date appearing over his shoulder from up on the street. She was blond and beautiful and probably perfect for him.

"She's waiting. Go, please. I'm fine."

Mats turned and lifted his hand, asking her to wait. Then he looked back, his hand still on her arm.

"Why did you come here?"

Just lie. Just make some shit up and get the fuck out of here!

Remi closed her eyes and dropped her head. She wanted to lie. She wanted to lie and run away and just try to get on with her life. But when she looked back into his eyes, she knew she couldn't. If nothing else, she had to tell him the truth.

"I came for you. I wanted to apologize and tell you that I...I'm an asshole. I should never have pushed you away, and I should've tried harder to keep you. After

London-" Her voice broke, and she felt him tense at the memory. "I should've tried harder to say I'm sorry. I should never have let you leave like that and-"

"Mats?" the woman called.

He turned and responded in Swedish, letting Remi go as he took a few steps closer. She looked pissed, and he didn't look any happier. She watched as he waved his hand around, pointing her way and shrugging. When he moved to the steps, to her, Remi knew she'd lost him.

Yeah. That's about right.

Turning her back on them, Remi started walking. The river was calm, and the sun was beginning to set. She wondered how long it would take to walk back to the hotel but knew it was way too far. Instead, she decided to walk a little bit closer to the city and then find a cab at the closest hotel.

Just keep walking. Take a bath. Get drunk. Go home. You were a fucking idiot to even think he'd still be into you, let alone single. It was three days, right? Not three years, so why-

"Remi, wait!"

She spun around to see him coming her way, an angry look on his face.

"Mats, I told you-"

"You're not making the rules here. OK? You show up after all these months, and now I have to explain to...to Eliza who you are and what you're doing here. She thought you were my wife and I was cheating."

Remi stammered an apology and shook her head. "So go! Go be with your girlfriend, and I'll go home. It's fine."

"Really? This shit again?"

When she looked into his eyes, all she saw was anger. It made her feel even worse to know that he not only didn't want her anymore but that he pretty much hated her.

"Remi, why are you here? Are you just here to fuck with me? What, you just sensed I was happy with someone new, and you decided to come and ruin it?"

"Mats, please," Remi tried, stepping back so she could gather her thoughts. "I…tried to move on from you, and it didn't take, OK? I've been fucking pining over you since I left and being here…I just needed to try."

"Try what?"

"To try and get you to forgive me. Because that guy in London - he was nothing. Literally, less than nothing. I was upset and missing you and angry that you hadn't called me back, so I went out looking for something to make myself feel better. And it didn't. I felt worse, right away, and then there you were, and I just-"

"I'm not mad about that, Remi. Yes, I was at the time because I was hurt and angry with myself. I hated the idea of anyone else touching you, but I shouldn't have walked away like that."

A lump formed in her throat, and she had to cough to steady her voice.

"I know I'm too late. And that's OK. I'm happy you're happy. I just…" She laughed and shook her head at the irony of it all. "I moved to Amsterdam to head up the new routes. And I guess being that close…I just hoped that maybe we could find a way to make this work. But I get it. I'm gonna be busy anyway, flying to Thailand, Japan, and Singapore. We're hoping to be in Australia in the next couple of years too, so…there's that to look forward to."

Mats stood still, his eyes on her as she spoke. She couldn't read his face, but he'd softened at least. Not quite so much hate in his eyes.

"I'm happy for you. Really I am. She's beautiful and probably way less messy than me." Remi stepped in and put her hand on his chest. "I'm just sorry I was too late."

She spun, tears brimming, heart aching, ready to walk away from the man she loved.

"Remi," he said softly catching her arm. "You might be a brilliant, world-wise pilot. But you really are an idiot with your heart."

She turned back and softened at his smile. "So I've been told."

Mats pulled her close and kissed her wet cheeks. "Amsterdam, huh? I think I could make that work."

THIRTY-NINE

Three Weeks Later

"Good morning, ladies and gentlemen, and welcome to Bangkok. The local time is 1:55 pm, and it's a very balmy 28 degrees outside. However, it looks like the weather is warming up, and we might be in for a storm later today. On behalf of everyone here at Atlântica Airway, thank you for choosing to fly with us. We hope to see you again on one of our flights soon."

"Do you think we can upgrade at the hotel? It's Lars and my six-month-matched anniversary, and I wanna surprise him with something romantic."

Remi rolled her eyes and sighed. "Young love. How sweet."

Chris frowned as they powered down the engine and started to check over their list. The flight was due to be refueled and turned around, so they would be off duty sooner rather than later.

"You can absolutely upgrade, and you know what, it's on me. I'm sure I still owe you for something, and at least I'll know you're nowhere near my room for your three-day sex session."

"Hey," he whined, playfully punching her arm. "It's his first time here, so we're planning on seeing as much as possible. Thanks again for getting him in First."

Remi shrugged and flipped her hair. "It pays to be the Queen."

Knowing Lars was waiting, Chris hustled through security. They met up in the baggage claim and found their car waiting. Remi made her way to the shuttle with the rest of the crew, hot, tired, and ready for a shower.

Since Chris and Lars would no doubt beat her to the hotel, she called ahead and asked for the upgrade, assuring them that yes, she wanted to upgrade someone else to a suite, and yes, she did want the lover's package.

Whatever the fuck that means.

On her own arrival, a lovely man appeared at her side with a fruity cocktail.

"From Mr. Chris," the man smiled.

She happily accepted the drink while she waited to check-in. The fans in the lobby were working overtime, but it was still crazy humid. Ten minutes later, Remi was happy to be in her air-conditioned room and out of her uniform.

But instead of changing into sweats and ordering room service, she slipped into a skimpy dress and made her way out into the afternoon heat. She tied her hair up to keep it off her back as she walked towards the Skytrain, the new heels not quite broken in but still sexy as hell.

The Bangkok Marriott, the Sukhumvit, was on the outskirts of the city, but it only took 20 minutes to reach Nana. From there, she walked through the noisy streets to Belga, a popular rooftop bar and restaurant with stunning city views.

With it still being kind of early, Remi found an empty seat near the glass, sitting with her back to the bar so she could see the city. She ordered the tuna tartare and crab bites, along with an Amara.

She'd ordered it last time she was there just for the tequila and had fallen in love. Now, a week later, she sipped with her eyes closed, waiting for the food with a grumble in her stomach.

"Hi," a deep voice said from her side. "You look kind of lonely over here by yourself."

Remi opened her eyes and looked up. With a smirk, she replied, "Lonely? Or blissfully content with my drink and own company."

He laughed and shrugged. "Not looking for company then?"

She sighed and waved her hand to the empty seat. "Why not?"

"Why not? Wow, so glad I came all this way."

The waiter, being extremely attentive, noticed the man without a drink and hustled over to take his order.

"Do you still have the Vedett Blond?" The waiter nodded and looked to Remi. "She'll have another, too."

He smiled at her and leaned over the table, his hand suddenly on her thigh and riding up to her crotch.

"If I didn't know any better, I'd say you were trying to get me drunk."

Mats grinned as his hand grazed her panties. "No. I don't want you drunk. I just want you buzzed and happy and up for anything."

Remi sat up and leaned into him, her tits pushing out as she brought her arms together. "Be careful. In Bangkok, that could mean something very different."

She lifted her butt until her lips met his. His tongue slipped into her mouth, and she felt his hand press against her mound.

Pulling back, she whispered, "Keep it in your pants. We've got food coming."

"I haven't seen you in a week. I don't know if I can wait that long."

He grinned and bit his lip, leaning back into his seat as the waiter brought over the drinks. Before he could leave, Remi put a hand on his arm.

"Sorry, we forgot something in our room. We'll be back in five minutes, so would you mind asking them to hold the food until then?"

"Of course, Miss." The kind man nodded and bowed, shuffling back so he could race to the kitchen.

"You've got five minutes. Make 'em count."

FORTY

Mats took her hand and pulled her to the elevator. They stood side by side, skin on skin, their arms hot and sweaty. When the doors finally opened, he all but threw her inside, pushing her against the back wall and capturing her mouth with his.

Remi wrapped her arms around his neck and drew back. "Hit the button."

Mats turned and smacked his hand on their floor before spinning back to her.

"You wore this to torture me, didn't you?"

"I might've."

His hands slid up her back and into her hair as she kissed her once more, lifting her up until she wrapped her legs around his waist. He tugged at the tiny strap holding her dress up but stopped as soon as the elevator dinged.

Remi dropped to her feet and adjusted herself, watching as the doors opened. When they saw the coast was clear, Mats lifted her over his shoulder and ran to the room.

The door was barely closed behind them before he had his hand up her skirt. He lifted the flimsy fabric over her head and tossed it over his shoulder, moving into her breasts like an animal.

He pulled the strap of her bra down, and she gasped when his lips touched her nipple. Remi fumbled with the button on his pants, pulling the fabric apart as she tried to free him.

"Take your fucking pants off," she ordered, turning her back on him and sashaying towards the big bed.

On the nightstand, she noticed a new toy. "You've been shopping?"

Mats grinned and rushed her, lifting her into his arms as they both fell onto the plush sheets. "It's for later," he growled, pinning her arms and finding her nipple once more.

Remi could already feel she was wet - she had been since she arrived at just the thought of seeing Mats. When he finally slipped his fingers under her panties, she felt his smile.

"Did you start without me?" he asked, gently caressing her, working around her clit.

"Maybe," Remi said, biting her lip.

Mats climbed up and kissed her as he moved his fingers inside. She let out a moan and grasped for his dick as he massaged her G-spot.

"Just fuck me," she breathed, not wanting to wait any longer.

He did as he was told, rolling over at her side so he could get out of his briefs. Remi took to opportunity to sit up and mount him, her slick pussy settling right on his thick shaft.

As she moved her hips, she leaned down and brushed her lips against his. His hands reached behind and undid her bra before scratching their way around and taking them in each hand. Finally, he moved to her nipples and pinched, twirling them in between his fingers, drawing a gasp from her lips.

As much as she wanted to draw it out, she'd been horny since she left. Leaving him for a week of meetings and massages while she flew a plane full of tourists home and waited for the turnaround.

She needed him fast. Playtime would have to wait.

Remi reached between them and lifted her hips. Guiding him inside, she cried out as he filled her. He slid in like butter, and she laughed at the relief she felt.

Mats reached his hand to her mouth and slid his fingers inside while she started to move. She sucked on them as she fucked him, desperate to feel them on her clit. When he pulled them free, he stopped at her nipple, pinching and tugging at it until she leaned down, putting her hand on his chest for support.

Finally, he found her clit. The shock she felt catapulted up to her nipples, and he instinctively lifted his other hand to meet them. Remi moved faster, squeezing him with everything she had.

They found their rhythm together, his fingers on her clit as she worked them both to the edge.

When her breathing became strained, Mats shifted his hips, pulling her to meet his lips. He grabbed at her and turned them both until he was positioned behind her. She fit into the curve of his body like she was made for it, and even as she twisted her torso to reach for his lips, he thrust inside, pulling a moan of pleasure from her spent lungs.

From the new angle, he had easy access to her tits and clit. He started slow, twisting and plucking at her until she growled his name. Then, as gently as he could, he traced his fingers over her mound.

The tickling sent chills up her spine. With his other hand stuck under her head, she reached for her breasts, teasing herself as he worked her harder and faster.

He let go briefly, pulling her leg to his chest, opening her sex for him completely. With the new access, he came in rough, dragging his fingers over her nub until she started to gasp. The harder her breaths came, the harder his fingers pressed. When she began to moan aloud, he spanked her, gently but firm enough to send a shock through her body.

She heard him breathing harder himself and breathed, "Harder, Mats. Please."

He did as he was told, ramming into her and slapping at her clit until she came in a wave of moans. His fingers stayed put but returned to more gentle circles as he thrust his hips a few more times, cumming hard and loud.

Mats shuddered and sighed, his breath short and his forehead sweaty.

"I think that was more than five minutes." He laughed.

"Who cares," Remi breathed, twisting onto her other side so she could look at him. But her eyes were drawn to the toy on the bedside table. "You gonna tell me what that is?"

She saw him grin as he reached back to grab it.

It was small, curved, pink, and silicone. When he pushed a button, it started to vibrate.

"You wear this. And I control it."

Remi lifted her eyebrow and took the thing in her hands. Clearly, the large end went in her pussy, and the slimmer part was for her clit. She twitched at the thought of it, her eyes widening as he grabbed the remote.

She felt it start to buzz faster in her hand; the pulses change with each push on the remote.

"You said you missed me. With this, I can make you come from across the fucking world."

Remi licked her lips and glanced at the clock. "I'm starved. What do you say we take this baby for a test drive?"

"You read my mind."

THANK YOU FOR READING

If you enjoyed the story, I hope you'll consider leaving a review!

Continue to the next page to find out about my second romance novel!

BOOKS BY THIS AUTHOR

Remodeling Romance

Stella's life is in bittersweet disarray. On the one hand, she's building her dream home. But she's also stuck in a dead-end relationship with Todd and can't stop fantasizing about a mysterious worker at her house— a man she calls "Dark Eyes."

But when Todd goes behind her back and changes something in the house, Stella finally snaps. She dumps Todd and fires the contractor, then soon finds herself being comforted by none other than Dark Eyes himself—Cal.

To her surprise, Cal offers to finish the house with his tall, toned, and sexy brothers, and things quickly heat up between them. Their secret, steamy affair is everything Stella's been craving. But it's not long before their romance is tested, and Stella isn't sure if they have what it takes to survive.

Packed with sizzling romance and heart-pounding action, this story of love and lust will keep you hooked until the very end.

Note: This book contains explicit sexual content and is perfect for mature romance readers.

Printed in Great Britain
by Amazon

57483995R10148